Story Times With Grandma

Mary Elizabeth Yoder

Christian Light Publications
Harrisonburg, Virginia 22802

MORE STORY TIMES WITH GRANDMA

Christian Light Publications, Inc., Harrisonburg, Virginia 22802

Printed in the United States of America

3rd Printing, 2006

Cover photo by Virginia Swartzentruber
Cover design by David Miller

ISBN-13: 978-0-87813-591-2
ISBN-10: 0-87813-591-X

TABLE OF CONTENTS

Section One

Section Two

SECTION ONE

All of the stories in this section actually happened to the author's family.

SLOW RIDE—FAST RIDE

Slowly, slowly, the old black car went *rattle, rattle, bump, bump* over the rough stones. A man held up a red flag, and Daddy stopped the car. A long string of cars passed in the other direction. Now the car could go a little way again. Now Daddy had to stop to let a big machine pass.

"I'm hot and sticky. I don't like this bumpy road. Let's go faster," begged tiny Linda.

"I think this is fun," said Wayne, the mechanic of the family. "I wish we would have to stop right beside one of those great big machines so I could watch it work."

Slowly they went on until Daddy saw a sign. "End of construction, resume speed," he read.

"Here we are, Linda," said Daddy. "See the nice smooth road ahead. That is what they are doing to the road back there. They will make it nice and smooth like this road." Daddy stepped on the gas, and the car seemed to fly after the slow bumpy ride.

"Give it the gas. Give it the gas. Step on it," cheered Wayne and Larry.

Daddy laughed. "Here we go," he said.

Suddenly a gray car with the letters, **P-O-L-I-C-E,** on the back shot past them.

"Say, that's a policeman," said Wayne, his eyes getting big and round. A siren sounded and the police car pulled to the side of the road. The signals flashed for Daddy to stop too.

"Well, I guess I went too fast," said Daddy, pulling off the road.

"Will he make you go to jail?" whispered Larry in a worried voice.

Kathy took a tight hold on Mother's arm. Linda put her arms around Mother's neck. Eight brown eyes were big with wonder.

The policeman climbed out of his car and walked over to Daddy's window. How tall he looked with his policeman's hat and suit. "May I see your driver's license, sir?" he asked.

Daddy reached into his pocket and pulled out his billfold. "Here it is, sir," he said.

"What model car is this?" asked the policeman.

"This is a 1988 Ford," replied Daddy. Mr. Policeman looked into the backseat and began to count. Then he looked into the front seat, three, four, five, six—six people in the car. "You mean to tell me you drive at 75 miles an hour with a nice family like that in an old car?"

he asked. "If you love your family, you should be more careful than that."

"Well, I certainly do love my family," answered Daddy. "And I am sorry I forgot to watch my speedometer."

Linda began to sob. Kathy stood up on the seat so she could get her arms around Mother's neck. Her hair tickled Mother's face. Larry's eyes blinked like the policeman's signal lights. Wayne's eyes were wide open.

"It's all right," Mother whispered in the girls' ears.

The policeman wrote Daddy's name down in a little green notebook. He took off his policeman's cap and put it back on his head, adjusting the strap under his chin. "I warn you, sir, that if I ever catch you again driving at that speed, it will mean more than merely talking to you. Watch your speedometer and take care of your family."

The policeman walked back to his car. With a wave of his hand and a friendly smile, he was gone.

Linda's hold on Mother's neck relaxed. Kathy sat down on the seat between Mother and Daddy. Wayne and Larry leaned back against the seat and sighed big sighs of relief.

"He didn't hurt us, did he? He was even a little bit friendly."

Daddy smiled and sighed. "No, he didn't hurt us. Policemen are here to help us, not to hurt us."

"I didn't like the policeman," said Linda.

"Why did he make you stop and scold you, Daddy?"

"Daddy needed to be scolded, dear," Daddy explained. "The Bible tells us to obey the laws. I should not have gone more than 60 miles an hour. That is the speed limit here. So you see, I was wrong, and Mr. Policeman was only doing his duty to make me stop."

Linda sighed a big, big sigh of relief. "I'm glad he didn't spank you," she said.

"Next time I will help you remember not to go too fast," said Kathy.

"That will be fine," laughed Daddy. "We want to obey the laws. When we go too fast, we make it dangerous for other people too."

Wayne was thoughtful. "I am glad for policemen who make people obey the laws."

KATHY'S GOOD-AS-NEW EAR

Tap, tap, tap. Mother tapped on the windowpane to tell Kathy lunch was ready. But Kathy didn't hear the tapping. She sat down on her little red sled and went for another ride.

The next time she came up the hill, Mother went out on the porch and called, "Kathy!" No answer. Then she called very loudly, "Kathy!"

Kathy looked up and came running toward Mother. She set the red sled up on the porch and swept the snow off her brown boots. Then she went into the house.

"My, what rosy cheeks you have! And your nose is as red as your tricycle. Are you cold?" Mother asked.

"Only my face," Kathy said, touching Mother's cheek with her warm hands. "These new green mittens keep my hands as warm as toast." Then she took her place at the table.

Daddy asked the blessing and everyone began to eat, that is, everyone but Kathy. She only nibbled, even though it was her favorite chicken dinner. She put her hand up against her right ear and looked very sober.

"Why don't you eat your lunch, dear?" Mother asked.

A big tear slipped from the corner of Kathy's eye, rolled down her cheek, and splashed right onto her plate. She poked her finger into her ear and said, "My ear hurts when I swallow."

"What? Is your ear hurting again? And I had to call you several times before you heard me." Mother laid her hand on Kathy's forehead. "You aren't hot, but I think we had better go see Dr. Tice this afternoon."

After lunch Kathy lay on the couch with a hot-water bottle on her ear while Mother washed the dishes. Then she changed into a Sunday dress and rode with Mother to Dr. Tice's office.

My, what a lot of sick babies there must be, thought Kathy as she looked around the waiting room full of people. One little boy about her size was crying. He kept saying, "I don't want to go in to the doctor. He will give me a shot."

Kathy looked at Mother and smiled. She knew Dr. Tice had to give shots sometimes, but he was such a nice, friendly doctor, and he did it so quickly that Kathy hardly found it out. "I'm not scared," she whispered.

Kathy watched the babies till her turn came. "Next," said Miss Brown.

Dr. Tice was wearing his white suit with the funny shirt that buttoned down the side. His friendly brown eyes twinkled when he said, "Hello, Kathy. How is my big girl today?"

"I'm fine except my ear hurts," Kathy answered. Sitting down in the swivel chair at his shiny desk, Dr. Tice began asking Mother lots of questions. Kathy looked all around the room. It smelled of medicines, alcohol, and adhesive tape just like it always did.

When the doctor couldn't think of another question to ask, he said, "Now let's see if we can find what is bothering my big girl." He popped a thermometer that tasted of alcohol into Kathy's mouth. While she held it under her tongue, he took his cold stethoscope and listened to her heart.

"Her heart's ticking fine and her temperature is normal," said Dr. Tice, looking at the thermometer. "Now let me see your throat," he said.

Kathy opened her mouth real wide. "Fine! I'd better be careful not to fall in there," he said laughing. "Now let's see your ears. Is this the one that's hurting you?"

"No, sir, it is the other one," Kathy answered. Dr. Tice looked into the other one. "Ooops! There's enough wax in there to wax your mommy's kitchen floor." Kathy giggled. Then he added, "I will have to wash it out."

Kathy's face grew sober, and her big brown

eyes blinked.

"Now, if you can get those pretty, red curls up out of the way so that they don't get wet, we will see what we can do," said the doctor.

Mother opened her purse and got some bobby pins. She pinned Kathy's hair tight against her head. Dr. Tice gave Mother a funny-shaped basin to hold against Kathy's cheek.

"Will it hurt?" Kathy asked in a worried voice.

"It won't hurt, but it will feel funny," promised Dr. Tice. Then he filled his syringe with warm water and squeezed it into Kathy's ear. *Swoosh, swish, splash, splash.* It sounded like a waterfall. Twice more he filled the syringe and squeezed. Out came a big piece of wax.

"There it is," said the doctor. "It's a wonder the child could hear." Then looking closer, he said, "It's not only wax; it's a piece of cotton encased in wax. How did that cotton get in there? Does it feel better, honey?"

Kathy wasn't sure. So he looked into her ear again. Then he showed her how to hold her ear so that the water could run out.

"That's all, and I don't think it will bother you any more." He set Kathy down on the floor and patted her hair. "I wish all my patients were as good as you were. I usually have to get Miss Brown in to help me when I have to do this. Here's a lollipop for being such a fine patient."

"Thank you," said Kathy as she walked

through the door with Mother. Outside she heard the snow saying *squeak, squeak,* when she stepped on it. A big train went rushing through town, its whistle blowing. Kathy held tightly to Mother's hand.

"I guess my ear is as good as new," she said. "Everything sounds so loud."

LARRY AND THE SALESMAN

Chubby Larry was making a road in the sandbox when he heard a car pull into the driveway. He watched a tall man get out of a green car and reach back for a briefcase. Dropping his shovel, Larry ran to the house. "Mother, there's a salesman coming," he called.

Larry stayed in the kitchen until the salesman was inside. The salesman was selling magazine subscriptions. *Oh, well, he won't give me chewing gum like the brush salesman,* Larry thought. *I'll go back outside to the sandbox and finish making my road.*

Coming outside, Larry saw Uncle Peter's cows grazing in the field right by the fence. Larry forgot the road he was making. He ran over to the fence, squatted down on the grass, and watched the cows taking big, big bites of green grass and flowering clover. *What would happen if they ate a flower with a honey bee on it?* he wondered.

After awhile the salesman came out of the house. He walked over to the fence and looked down at Larry. "Don't you think those cows will notice you are a pretty fat boy and think you might taste better than grass?" he asked.

Larry's big, brown eyes flew wide open. He scooted away from the fence and looked at the salesman to see if he was teasing. The salesman looked serious. "If I were as chubby as you are I wouldn't get too close to those big mouths," he added. Then he chuckled, walked to his car, and drove away with a friendly wave.

Larry scooted farther away from the fence and watched the cows' big jaws grab big mouths full of clover and gobble them down. Suddenly a huge black-and-white Holstein poked her nose under the fence, stretched her long, red tongue around a clover plant, and ripped it into her mouth.

Larry jumped up and ran to the porch. Soon another cow reached under the fence and grabbed a clover plant. Larry saw how long their jaws were. "They just might see that I am pretty chubby," he decided. "I'll go into the house and stay there till Wayne comes home from school."

Larry slowly walked into the sewing room and stood by Mother, watching the needle bobbing up and down in Kathy's new dress.

Mother looked at Larry questioningly. "Are you finished playing in the sandpile?" she asked.

"I'm going to wait till Wayne comes home from school to finish my road. When will Linda and Kathy wake up?"

"I hope they will sleep at least another half hour," Mother answered.

"What can I do now?" Larry wanted to know. "Why don't we go out and work in the garden till Wayne comes home from school?"

Mother looked at Larry in surprise. "I thought you didn't like helping me in the garden," she said. "It's too wet to work in the garden. Remember it rained yesterday."

"Tell me a story, then," begged Larry. But just then the phone rang, and by the time Mother had finished talking with Aunt Helen, Kathy and Linda were awake.

"Let's go outside and play in the sand," Kathy suggested.

"Oh, it's hot out there. Let's wait till Wayne comes home from school," stammered Larry.

Mother looked at Larry with a puzzled expression and wondered why her bouncy, outdoor-boy didn't want to go outside.

When Wayne came home, all the children trooped out to the sandbox. Larry stayed far away from the fence and kept Kathy and Linda close to the sandbox. *If the cows would like me they might like my little sisters too,* he thought.

For the next several weeks, Larry refused to play outside when the cows were in the pasture, unless Mother, Daddy, or Wayne were with him. Mother talked to Daddy about Larry's strange behavior when Larry was sleeping. "I just can't understand what came over our sunny, little outdoor-boy. I didn't find out that the cows did anything to frighten him, but he acts scared."

"Maybe we should take the children over to Uncle Peter's some evening when they are milking so that Larry can get better acquainted with the cows," Daddy suggested.

The next evening the family drove over to Uncle Peter's to watch the milking. Larry was fascinated as Helen washed the cows' udders and Peter put the milking machines on them. His eyes grew big and round when he saw the milk draw up into the clear plastic pipes and rush out to the milk house.

When they went into the feeding room where they could watch the cows eat, Larry took a very tight hold on Daddy's hand. Suddenly a cow stretched out her long tongue to reach something in Larry's direction. Larry jumped back so that he hit his head on the manger behind him. Tugging on Daddy's hand he exclaimed, "Let's get out of here. Those cows might see that I'm pretty nice and fat."

Uncle Peter, who didn't know about Larry's fear, put his head back and laughed a big rolling laugh. Larry hid behind Daddy's trouser leg.

Daddy gently led him out of the feeding room where he felt safer. Squatting down he pulled Larry close, and explained, "Larry boy, cows eat only grasses and grains. What made you think they would eat little boys?"

Larry blinked back tears. "Tha . . . that m . . . man, that salesman said I'd better stay away from the fence 'cause the cows might see that I'm nice and fat," he stuttered.

Daddy shook his head. "The salesman was only teasing you, Larry," he explained.

"Th . . . then they won't hurt me if I sit out by the fence and watch them eat grass?" Larry wanted to know.

"Certainly not," Daddy said.

Larry's eyes sparkled and a smile spread over his chubby face. He let go of Daddy's hand and ran back to the feeding room to watch the cows enjoy their grain supper.

APPLES, APPLES, APPLES

Daddy pushed his chair back from the supper table. "Uncle Donald has more apples than he can harvest. He offered us all we want to make apple butter if we gather them," he said.

Four pairs of brown eyes sparkled. "Yummy, yummy, apple butter. We like apple butter bread," exclaimed Wayne, Larry, Kathy, and Linda.

"Good," said Daddy. "And who will help me gather the apples?"

"I will. I will," shouted slim Wayne, scooting out of his chair.

"Me, me," shouted chubby Larry bouncing out of his chair.

"Me too," added Kathy with the red hair.

"I'll help," said Mother, hurrying to clear the table.

Little Linda's eyes stopped sparkling, and her pretty dimples disappeared. She just sat in her chair and didn't say one word.

"Fine," said Daddy. "I'll get some baskets and bags to put the apples in while you barefooted children get your shoes on."

Everyone was so busy that no one noticed Linda still sitting in her chair. Finally she hopped down and followed Mother. Clinging to her skirts, she begged, "Mommy, stay here with me."

Mother looked down at the sober little face in surprise. "Don't you want to help gather apples?" she asked.

Linda's chin quivered, and a salty tear slid down one rosy cheek. "W . . . will it get dark?" she asked.

Stooping, Mother drew Linda close and glanced at the clock. "It probably will before we get back. But the moon will be shining, and Daddy and I will be right there," she promised.

Linda sighed a big sigh and rubbed the tears out of her eyes with her fists.

"Everybody ready?" Daddy called.

"We're coming," Mother answered. She took Linda's hand as they went outside. In a short time their pickup truck stopped in Uncle Donald's orchard between rows of loaded apple trees.

Uncle Donald walked out from the barn to say hello.

"We took you up on your offer, and I brought the whole family along to help," Daddy laughed.

"Fine," exclaimed Uncle Donald. "I'd much rather have you use the apples than let them go to waste. Take all you can use for winter too. I'd help, but I have chores to finish." Then he went back to the barn.

"All right; let's get started," said Daddy. "I'll shake this tree. Then I can pick some good solid apples while you pick up the apples I shook down."

Up, up, up into the tree went Daddy. Only his old, black hat and patched denims showed between the leaves and branches of the tree. "All set," Daddy called. "Now look out!"

Suddenly apples came thumping down in every direction. Linda's brown eyes sparkled, and her dimples showed. "Whheee! Daddy is making it rain apples," she laughed.

When the apples stopped falling, everyone began to pick them up. *Plunk, plunk,* apples went into Mother's and the boys' middle-sized buckets. *Plink, plink,* they went into Kathy's and Linda's little buckets. *Clang, clang,* they landed in Daddy's big bucket.

Daddy handed big red apples down to Mother from the tree he was picking. Kathy and Linda raced over to hold a bag so that Mother could pour the apples into it. Then they scampered back to pick up more apples.

After a while Mother called, "We'll have to stop. All our bags and baskets are filled." Daddy jumped down from the tree. "Mother, you and the girls can rest on that log while the boys help me load the apples," he suggested.

"We can deliver them to the apple butter factory first thing in the morning."

Mother sat on the log with Kathy and Linda snuggled against her. Linda laid her head in Mother's lap and looked up, astonished. "Oh, see the moon and the stars! When did it get dark?"

Mother smiled. "Quite a while ago, but you were too busy to notice."

When the apples were loaded, Daddy and the boys came over to rest too. "Listen to the night sounds," Daddy said.

"I hear the katydids arguing whether Katy did or didn't," chuckled Larry.

"I hear a frog saying 'Cr-r-r-onk, cr-r-r-onk,' " said Wayne.

A killdeer flew across the meadow calling, "Kill deer, kill deer, kill deer."

"Moo," said a cow close by.

"Maa," answered her calf from the stable.

"That was mommy and her baby talking to each other," Linda said.

"The cricket's song is slow this evening because it's cool," Daddy remarked.

"Let's have our evening devotions here," Kathy suggested.

"Yes, let's," Linda sighed. "I like the sounds and the lights in the night," she said.

GARDEN FUN

Thump! Larry jumped out of bed and looked out the window. He quickly pulled on his blue jeans and ran downstairs. "It's such a nice day. Let's go fishing and have a picnic," he begged.

"That would be nice," Daddy agreed. "But don't you think we had better plant some seeds in the garden today? Perhaps we can go fishing while the seeds grow."

Larry frowned. "That won't be any fun," he grumbled.

After breakfast, Daddy and Wayne went out to the garden and began picking up stones. *Clatter, rattle, bang,* they threw them into the wheelbarrow.

Larry sat on the porch with his head in his hands. A big frown had replaced his usual sunny smile. "Why do we have to stay at home and work on Saturdays when most boys are having fun?" he grumbled to himself.

Father Wren flew down and sat on the wash line with a twig in his mouth. He cocked his head from one side to the other and blinked his tiny, black eyes at Larry. "Ch-ch-ch," he scolded. Mother Wren came out of the little birdhouse on the porch. She took the twig and hurried back into her house.

Larry just sat there pouting.

Father Wren began singing his cheery little song, his throat quivering. Larry looked up to see how so much noise could come from such a little bird.

What does he have to sing about? All he does is work, work, work, thought Larry.

Father Wren flew away and brought another twig for Mrs. Wren. Then he sang until his throat quivered again.

Larry's eyes began to twinkle as he watched and listened. Suddenly he jumped up. "I guess I'll go and help Daddy," he said.

The sun shone very warm. Larry's chubby arms grew tired, and his back ached. He took Daddy's big red handkerchief and wiped the sweat from his flushed face.

"I wish I were fishing," he complained. Just then he saw a fishing worm under a stone. "Here is a fishing worm," he shouted. "Shall I kill him?"

"No, don't kill him," Daddy said. "He won't harm anyone. But he will help keep the soil in good condition."

"He would make good fishing bait too," said Wayne.

After a while all the stones were gone from the small garden. Mother, Kathy, and Linda came out to help.

"Now I will make some rows," said Daddy. "Then you can help Mother drop in the seeds and cover them with soft earth."

Daddy and the boys went to take stones off the big garden.

"Here's an old cornstalk," called Larry.

"Pull it out," said Daddy.

Larry pulled and tugged and tugged and pulled. Suddenly, out came the cornstalk. Down went Larry, right on his back. How funny he looked with his feet in the air, still clutching that old cornstalk. Everybody laughed and laughed.

Larry jumped up, grinning. "That was fun," he said. "Where's another one?"

Soon all the children were pulling cornstalks, rolling over, and laughing as they rolled.

After lunch everyone rested—that is, everyone except Father Wren. He sat on the wash line and sang.

"My, my!" said Larry. "Don't wrens ever rest?" Then he jumped up. "Come on. Let's get back to work."

Mother smiled at Daddy. "He seems to have forgotten about fishing," she whispered.

Back to the garden they trooped.

"Now we will plant the peas," planned Mother. "You may help drop them into the rows, children."

Linda was in such a hurry that she fell down. She cried when she saw the dirt on her blue dress. Mother began to brush it off.

Suddenly Linda laughed. "I thought I was hurt, but I'm not. The ground is as soft as Mama's cushions."

"Will we plant sweet corn?" Larry asked.

"I'm afraid it will freeze if we do," said Mother, "but we will plant a little bit. Then if it doesn't freeze, we will have some real early corn."

When the peas and corn were planted, Daddy began to make some deep furrows that looked like little ditches. "These are for potatoes," he said.

Kathy's eyes grew big and round. "Where are the potato seeds?" she asked.

Mother took a potato with a red skin and showed Kathy and Linda the little spots on it. "We call those spots the potato eyes," she explained. "A new plant grows from each of the eyes, so I will cut the potatoes into pieces. Then we will have several plants from one potato."

"Oh," said Kathy, "God knows how to make everything just right."

The children put the potatoes into the furrows, and Daddy covered them with the brown earth.

"Well, I guess that's all for now," he said. "We will have another planting day when the danger of frost is past."

Four tired, dirt-streaked children went to

the house and got cleaned up for supper.

After supper when the children were getting into their pajamas, Father Wren sang his last evening song.

Larry sighed, "I wonder if Father Wren is as tired as I am," he said. "But he isn't too tired to sing."

Daddy read a Bible story to a sleepy audience. Linda snuggled into Mother's arms and was soon fast asleep.

Prayers were said. Sleepily, Larry prayed, "Thank You, God, for Mother and Daddy. Thank You for wrens that sing. Thank You for gardens and stones to haul. And thank You for cornstalks to pull, and just everything that made this a good day, even though I couldn't go fishing. Amen."

"Amen," said Mother and Daddy.

BOSSY SAMPLES THE GARDEN

Wayne and Larry were hoeing corn in their family garden. Larry flopped right down in the middle of the cornrow. "My back's breaking," he said. "It's too hot to work. Let's quit."

Wayne leaned on his hoe handle. "Come on and help," he demanded. "You're just lazy. Think how good this corn will taste. See, it won't be long anymore. It's almost as tall as I am, and here it's coming into tassels too."

Chubby Larry didn't budge. He just blinked his big, brown eyes and drew a picture in the dust. "I don't care. My two front teeth won't be big enough to eat much corn on the cob anyway. But I sure hope I can handle some of it."

Right on the other side of the garden fence, Farmer Joe's cows grazed every night. Most of the cows were good cows. But Bossy had one dreadful fault; she was dissatisfied. Even if she was in clover up to her knees, she kept looking across the fence at the good things that grew in the garden.

One night when everyone was fast asleep, she reached across the fence and took a taste of that corn. How good it was. With a little pushing and a few scratches, she was right in the garden. She ate up every bit of the early corn and snipped the tops off the late corn.

The next morning when the children looked out the window and saw the corn was gone, they were very upset!

"After all the work we did, and it was almost ready to eat," Wayne grumbled. "I think Bossy is a mean, old cow!"

"Why didn't she go and eat the corn in Farmer Joe's field?" Larry wanted to know.

Daddy asked the blessing as though nothing had happened.

"Don't you even care, Daddy?" Wayne asked.

"Oh, yes, I'm sorry," Daddy admitted. "But when I think of the many children in the world who are hungry and have no garden at all, losing a little corn doesn't seem so bad. We still have plenty to eat."

Wayne's eyes softened as he thought of the children in Virginia who had lost everything in a flood. But then his eyes began to snap again. "That may be true, but I still think Bossy is a mean cow," he stormed. Then he thought a little. "Last Sunday our memory verse said, 'All things work together for good to them that love God.' Miss Brown said there is some good in nearly everything that happens if we look for it. But I don't see how there could be anything good in Bossy eating our sweet corn."

Since it was Sunday, Daddy asked Farmer Joe to keep Bossy in the stable until he could fix the fence. The children were glad to think Bossy was being punished. Monday evening right after supper Daddy went to fix the fence. Wayne brought wire and tools from the garage.

Before the fence was finished, the forty cows came into their night pasture. "Moo, moo," said Bossy, and she came right over to look around.

"Get out! Get out! Hey there, get out!" shouted the boys. Bossy wasn't alarmed by their noise. She stepped away and mooed loudly. Wayne and Larry jumped in surprise. Kathy's red pigtails bobbed as she ran closer to Daddy. Linda's brown eyes grew round as a cherry, and she took hold of Daddy's trouser leg.

Before long Bossy came into the garden. All the boys' shouting did not excite her. But when Daddy ran toward Bossy, waving his arms and shouting, Bossy turned and ran as fast as her legs would carry her.

Everybody laughed so loudly that Mother, who was washing dishes in the kitchen, hurried to the door to see what had happened.

She got to the door just in time to see Bossy gallop out of the garden. How she did laugh.

After running a little distance, Bossy stood and stared for a long time. Finally she said, "Moo," and walked to the other cows.

Linda ran into the house. "Daddy scared Bossy. Then she ran away and told the other cows what happened to her," she told Mother.

When the fence was finished, the family sat on the cool lawn to enjoy the moon and stars.

Wayne was thoughtful. "I believe I got some good out of Bossy getting into the garden after all. We had the fun of fixing the fence and seeing Daddy chase a cow."

"Is there anything else?" Daddy asked.

"Yes, it will give my teeth more time to grow till the corn is ready," said Larry.

Daddy smiled. "Yes," he agreed, "but isn't there something else?"

"I know," said Wayne. "It reminded us to remember our blessings and think of the children who don't have any garden and can't afford to buy food either."

"Right," said Daddy. "Shall we have our family devotions out here in the moonlight? We can sing 'Count Your Many Blessings,' name some blessings we are especially thankful for, and say Bible verses."

"Yes, lets!" agreed everyone.

What verse do you suppose Wayne said? He said, "All things work together for good to them that love God." And he knew that it was true.

WHERE'S SNOWBALL?

"Kitty, kitty, kitty," called Wayne. Fluff and Muff scurried off the porch to get their breakfast. Wayne looked around. "Kitty, kitty, Snowball, here's your breakfast," he shouted.

Wayne went back to the kitchen. "Mother, where's Snowball?" he asked. "She didn't come for breakfast. Have you seen her, Larry?"

Larry shook his head. Mother said, "I don't know. She didn't come for supper last evening either."

"Oh, Mother," Larry whimpered, "do you think a car ran over her? She was such a nice cat."

Just then Snowball leaped up on the window and said, "Meow!"

Both boys jumped. "Where did she come from?" Wayne asked, looking out the window. "She's hungry and the breakfast is all gone."

He warmed up some milk and took it out for

Snowball. She lapped it up, then hurried away behind the chicken house and disappeared. Try as they would, the boys could not find her.

Mother smiled a knowing smile when the boys told her she was gone. "I think Snowball has a secret," she said. "I saw her dash across the road and up to the woods."

Every day Snowball came late for meals and disappeared as soon as she had eaten. "Let's follow her and see where she goes," Wayne suggested one morning.

Larry ran into the house to tell Mother where they were going. By that time Snowball was far ahead. The boys climbed the fence and ran up through the field. Snowball was just at the edge of the woods when she saw them coming. Now she sat down on a big rock and began washing herself. She washed and washed. She blinked her big, yellow eyes at Wayne as if to ask, "What do you want?" then began washing again.

Larry shifted from one foot to the other. "She's not going anywhere, and I'm tired," he grumbled. "Come on. Let's go home."

"Yes, let's," Wayne agreed. "Let her keep her secret. We don't want to stand here and watch her wash herself all day."

Mother was surprised to see them back so soon. "I think you gave up too quickly," she said, smiling. "Remember the proverb 'If at first you don't succeed, try, try, again!' "

The next morning Wayne and Larry followed Snowball very carefully so that she would not see them. But Snowball was also more careful. She saw them coming and sat down to wash herself again. Finding seats on an old log, the boys rested while they watched her pink tongue cleaning her already white coat from top to bottom. Snowball kept blinking her eyes at them with a worried look.

A squirrel scolded from a tree, and a blue jay said, "Thief, thief." Snowball didn't care. She curled up to take a nap.

"Isn't she ever going anywhere?" asked Larry. "I'm thirsty. Come on. Let's go home."

"You may go if you like," Wayne answered. "I'm going to stay here until Snowball leaves."

Just then Snowball got up, yawned, and stretched a long, cat stretch. Then she started down across the hill through the woods. Around trees, under bushes, and over logs she went. Blackberry briers scratched Wayne and Larry as they followed. Suddenly Snowball disappeared behind a big rock.

The boys scrambled up on the rock, hoping to see her again. "Ouch," cried Larry, stooping to wipe blood from a long scratch on his leg. His chubby face was flushed and his eyes snapped. "Snowball's gone. Let's go home and let her keep her old secret."

Wayne rubbed a painful scratch of his own. "I'm not giving up yet," he decided. "Come. We'll circle back to the log where we started."

Larry followed, mumbling about his scratches.

Wayne headed straight for the log to sit

down and rest. "Oh, Larry, look here!" Larry hurried to see. Two white, one gray, and one yellow kitten were snuggled around Snowball in a little hollow under the log.

"You wise old cat," chuckled Wayne. "We were nearly sitting on your secret. You purposely led us away from it."

"Shall we take them home?" Larry asked. Wayne hesitated. "Let's go ask Mother," he said finally.

Kathy and Linda were all excited when they heard the boys had found Snowball's kittens. "Yes, yes, do bring them home. We want to see them too," they begged.

Mother thought a moment. "Snowball was using her God-given instinct for protecting her babies from enemies when she hid them," she explained. "But of course she does not think of the danger of crossing the highway. Besides, the weather is to turn cold and rainy. So take this basket and bring the kittens down to the garage."

The boys hurried back to the kittens. "Aren't they cute?" Wayne's black eyes sparkled. "Let's call them Buzz, Fuzz, Suzz and Agamemnon like the four little kittens in our book."

Gently the boys began putting them into the basket. Frightened, the kittens said, "Sptt, sptt, sptt." Their tiny tails grew big as bottle-brushes. Wayne and Larry laughed and laughed.

Snowball did not like the basket ride. She

jumped out and ran along behind the boys saying, "Meow, meow, meow." She sounded worried.

In the garage the boys fixed a box with soft hay and gently put the kittens into it. Snowball jumped right into it and began purring loudly to show how happy she was.

Mother, Kathy, and Linda hurried out to see the kittens. "Goody, goody, we're glad you brought them in. Oh, they're cute! The yellow one is prettiest of all," the girls exclaimed.

"Indeed they are cute," agreed Mother. "Now we had better leave Snowball alone with them so that she doesn't take them back to the woods."

The next morning it was raining, and a chilly breeze was stirring. Wayne and Larry ran out to see the kittens snug and warm in the garage. Wayne's teeth chattered. He looked at Larry hunching his shoulders to keep warm.

"I'm glad we didn't give up till we found the secret," Wayne said. "The kittens would be all wet and cold now if they were under that log."

Larry shivered and looked at his scratched arms, red with the Mercurochrome Mother had put on the scratches. "Me too," he said. "I didn't like the scratches. But I'm so glad the kittens are inside."

THE HORRID SPLINTER

Barefoot Wayne and Larry were playing hide-and-seek in the backyard. “Ready or not, you will now be caught,” called Wayne.

Larry, who was crouching behind the woodpile, decided to move back one more step. Suddenly he screamed, “OUCH! Ooo, ooww, oow, ouch!”

Wayne had no trouble finding him. He ran straight toward the noise. “What happened? What’s wrong?” he asked.

Larry hopped up and down on one foot. “A splinter! A splinter, a horrid splinter in my foot,” he cried.

With Wayne’s help Larry hopped into the house on one foot. How he screamed. Kathy awoke from her afternoon nap. Frightened by all the fuss, she began to cry too.

Mother turned off the washer and rushed up the steps two steps at a time. “Whatever is the matter?” she asked.

"Ouch! There's a horrid splinter in my foot," sobbed Larry.

Mother picked Larry up and set him on the table to see what horrid splinter would cause him to fuss so loudly. She turned on the light and stooped for a good look. The puzzled look on her face changed to sympathy. "You don't have a splinter in your foot, Larry. You have a bee sting."

Chubby Larry wiggled around on the table. "It stings, it hurts! Take it out!" he sobbed.

"Get the first aid kit, Wayne," Mother directed. "Now, Larry, sit still. I'll have it out in a jiffy and it will soon feel better."

Kathy who had climbed out of bed to see what all the fuss was about, stood beside Wayne and watched open-mouthed. Mother carefully scraped the stinger out to avoid squeezing the poison out of the little sac at its base. She made a thick paste of baking soda and water, heaped some on the spot, and tied a damp cloth around it.

In a few minutes, Larry stopped sobbing, but his big brown eyes snapped. "I hate bees!" he announced. "What are they good for? All they do is go buzz, buzz, buzz and sting little boys."

"Don't you know?" asked Wayne. "They give us honey. Don't they, Mother?"

"That's right," Mother agreed. "And who likes honey bread at our house?"

"Me," said Larry rubbing his chubby middle. "But I'll never go barefoot again."

"Making honey isn't all bees do for us,"

Mother continued. "They seldom sting unless they are bothered. Mr. Bee was only defending himself when you stepped on him. His stinger has little barbs on it, so he can't pull it out again when he stings. It tears out of his body and the bee dies."

Larry's eyes grew thoughtful. "What else do they do for us?" he asked.

Mother settled onto the couch with Kathy on her lap and the boys beside her. "When bees gather nectar to make honey, they carry pollen from one flower to another. We say they pollinate the flowers. When blossoms are not pollinated, they drop off and there's no fruit. Bees help give us apples, pears, cherries, and all the fruits you like so well."

"Do all bees gather nectar?" Wayne wanted to know.

"No," said Mother. "There are different kinds of bees. Only the workers gather nectar. The queen bee does nothing but lay eggs. The young workers take care of her and feed her. The young workers are nurse bees for the babies. They feed them and keep the hive clean. By fanning their wings when it gets too warm, they keep the right temperature in the hive. When it gets too cold, they crowd around the cells where the eggs and larvae are and keep them warm with their body heat."

"My, how do they know to do that?" Larry asked.

"It's what we call their God-given instinct," Mother explained. "That makes them know how to do things in a certain way."

"How do they gather the nectar and pollen?" Wayne asked.

"They gather the nectar with their mouths and store it in their bodies till they reach the hive," said Mother. "Other workers take the nectar and make it into honey and put it into combs in the hive. They carry the pollen in little baskets on their back legs. They scrape the pollen off the front and center legs into the little baskets. The workers in the hives take the pollen and store it in cells till they need it for food."

"Do all bees work?" Kathy asked.

"Drones, or father bees, do not work and they have no stingers," Mother explained. "When there are too many drones in the hive, the workers drive them out or sting them to death."

Larry's eyes grew big and round. "I'm glad I'm not a drone bee," he exclaimed.

Mother smiled. "I am too," she agreed. "But bees are one of God's most interesting creatures. They have special organs, or plates to make wax, which they form into the combs where the honey is stored."

Wayne's eyes sparkled. "My, I never knew that bees were such interesting creatures. Let's get a book at the library and see what else we can learn about them."

"Yes, let's," agreed Larry. "I know plenty about bee stings, but now I'd like to know more about bees."

THE LITTLE LOST LAMB

Larry bounced off the big yellow school bus and skipped toward the house. Suddenly he stopped and cocked his head. What was that noise?

"Baa, baa, baa." He heard it again. Dropping his lunch bucket and books on the porch, Larry hurried behind the house.

"Baa-aa." There was the sound again, even more pitiful than before.

Larry peered back through Farmer Yoder's maple grove to see where the sound came from. There were no sheep in sight. "Baaa." Then Larry saw it, a wee lamb huddled against a giant maple tree. How tiny and helpless it looked!

Larry turned and dashed back to the house and up the steps two at a time. Bursting into the kitchen, he called, "Mother, there's a wee lamb back in the grove all by itself."

Mother stopped squeezing red frosting out

of the cake decorator onto the cookie she was frosting and walked to the playroom window to see. Sure enough, there stood the wee lamb hunched up to keep warm in the cool, spring breeze.

"Well," she said, "the sheep had all been up in the pasture. Maybe this lamb was too tired to walk home."

"Poor little thing," said Larry. "I'll take him home. I'll catch him and carry him back to Mr. Yoder's farm."

"All right," Mother agreed. "If his mother has twins, she may not miss her lamb. Change your clothes, and you may go."

Quickly Larry changed into his old patched blue jeans and jacket. He dashed outside and ran to the pasture, shouting, "I'll take you home, little lost lamb."

The little lamb was frightened. Bleating loudly, he ran around the maple tree. Larry chased and tried to catch him, but the little lamb managed to keep just out of his reach.

Larry tripped over a root and went sprawling in the wet grass. Jumping up, he brushed the mud off his clothes. *It's good I changed clothes,* he thought.

Once more he started the chase. Grab, miss, grab, miss, around and around the tree they went. Larry's cheeks grew rosy and perspiration came out on his forehead. He unzipped his jacket and pushed back his red cap.

"You silly little lamb, I want to help you," he

shouted. The lamb bleated and kept just ahead of him. At last Larry stopped and pulled out his red bandanna to wipe his dripping face.

"All right, if you won't let me catch you, you can just stay right here," he snapped. Turning, he stamped back toward the house.

"Baa-aa," cried the little lamb. Larry stopped and looked back. The little lamb was panting and trembling.

"Poor little thing. You're scared, aren't you?" Sitting down, Larry spoke softly to the little animal. "I won't hurt you, lambkin. I want to help you. Come, pretty lamb."

The little lamb stood still and cried, "Baa, baa."

"Baa," Larry answered and slowly inched toward the lamb. "Nice lamb, nice little lamb, baa," he coaxed. At last he could reach him. With a quick sweep of his arms, Larry picked him up. Bleating in fright, the lamb struggled to get down. Larry held on, stroking and speaking gently to him. Soon the little lamb relaxed and snuggled down in his arms.

Holding the lamb gently, Larry trudged back through the grove, up a hill, and down the other side to the Yoder farm. Tired and lonely, the little lamb snuggled against him. Mr. Yoder saw them coming.

"Well, well," he exclaimed. "Here comes Larry, the shepherd boy, bringing a lost lamb home. A good shepherd you are, Larry."

Larry grinned as he told Mr. Yoder where he found the lamb. *He might not think I'm a good shepherd if he had seen me racing around that tree,* he thought.

"The sheep are in the pasture behind the barn," said Mr. Yoder. "Bring the lamb, and we'll find his mother."

Larry followed him to the pasture. His big eyes grew bigger when he saw the large flock of sheep. They all looked alike to him. "How will we ever know which is the little lost lamb's mother?" he wondered.

"One of the ewes seemed uneasy when I penned them in here," Mr. Yoder explained. "But she had one lamb with her; so I didn't pay much attention."

Just then one of the mother sheep raised her head and said, "Baa." The little lamb in Larry's arms struggled to get down. Larry set him down. Away ran the lamb as fast as his wobbly legs could carry him, straight to the mother sheep. He bounced under her and started drinking his supper. Mother sheep sniffed him, then his twin brother, and made a contented sound.

Larry laughed. "They think their supper is good," he said.

Mr. Yoder reached into his pocket. "What do I owe you for bringing the lamb home, Larry?" he asked.

Larry really hadn't been thinking about pay. He hooked his right thumb into his pocket and squinted his eyes the way he did when he was thinking real hard. *Some pay would help out on that bat I'm saving for. Besides it was worth something to Mr. Yoder to get his lamb back,* he thought.

"Here's a dollar. Is that enough?" asked Mr. Yoder, holding out a shiny new dollar bill.

Larry looked at the money, and then at the lambs delightfully wiggling their tails over their good supper. Suddenly he stood straight up. "I don't want anything," he said. "Not one cent. Seeing how happy the lamb and his mother are to be together again is enough pay for me."

"Well, thank you very much," smiled Mr. Yoder.

"You're welcome," answered Larry. With a happy, warm feeling in his heart he trudged back up the hill toward home.

SOMETHING SCARY

Kathy smoothed her red hair back securely and sat down at the little red table in the playroom. "I'm going to color the squirrel in my new coloring book," she announced. Linda tossed back her long, brown pigtails. "I'll color the kitten in mine," she planned. Their heads bent over their books as they carefully outlined their pictures.

Suddenly, a large, dark shadow crossed the table. Crash, something hit the window by the table. Kathy jumped, making a brown streak right through the grass in her picture. Linda's hand jerked, making her kitten's tongue black.

"What was that?" they asked in one breath. Together they jumped up and ran out to the kitchen. Kathy clung to Mother's skirt. "A scary thing crashed into the window and we saw a shadow go over the table," she exclaimed.

"What was it, Mother? It was scary," added Linda.

Mother dusted the flour off her hands and slid a pan of cookies into the oven. "I heard a noise, but I didn't see anything," she said. "Where did the noise seem to come from?"

"It was at the window," said Kathy, still hanging onto mother's skirt. She let go and stood back when Mother walked to the playroom and looked out the window.

"I can't see a thing," Mother said. "Are you sure the noise was at the window?"

"Yes," agreed the girls. "And the scary black shadow crossed the table at the same time."

Mother walked to the door and looked at the sunbeams dancing on the porch. "I don't see anything scary out here," she said. Then she opened the door and looked on the porch by the window.

"Oh, now I see what it was," she exclaimed. "A bird flew against the window, and his shadow must have crossed the table. He's completely knocked out."

Quickly she stepped outside and picked him up. "I'll bring him in so that Snowball won't get him."

"Let's see. Let's see," clamored the girls.

"Is he hurt?" asked Kathy.

Mother held the bird carefully, but his head hung limply, and he didn't move. She lifted one wing and parted the white feathers beneath it. "He's probably just stunned from flying against the window," she explained. "See, he's breathing and his tiny heart is beating. He may be all right in a little while."

"What kind of bird is it?" Linda asked.

"It's a red-headed woodpecker," Mother answered. "See the white markings on his wings and tail and his sharp bill. That helps him peck insects out of tree bark. And notice how red his head is. He really has the right name."

Linda adjusted her glasses and leaned forward to take a closer look. "Oh, the poor thing. He's so pretty," she exclaimed. "Can't we do something to make him get well?"

"Let's put Vaseline on his head. Maybe that would make it feel better," Kathy suggested.

Mother smiled. "I don't think Vaseline would help," she said. "But the Bible tells us that not one sparrow will fall without God's knowing about it, and I'm sure He knows about this woodpecker's accident. If the bird does come to, it will frighten him to be in the house. I will take him outside and put him up in the bird feeder where Snowball can't reach him. You can watch from the window to see what happens."

Mother took Mr. Woodpecker outside and laid him in the bird feeder. Then she hurried back to the kitchen to get her cookies out of the oven.

Kathy and Linda flattened their noses against the window to watch. Suddenly the woodpecker began to kick his feet in the air. "Mother! Mother, come quickly. He's moving," squealed Kathy.

Just as Mother came in, Mr. Woodpecker

got to his feet. His head wobbled from side to side, and he seemed unable to keep his balance. A bit later he hopped to the edge of the feeder and cocked his head with a puzzled expression. His eyes seemed to be getting brighter, and he held his head quite steadily.

"I think he's going to be all right," Mother decided. "He was only stunned. God saw it all and healed him. I hope he doesn't try to come through a closed window again."

"Me too," added Kathy. "It's too scary!"

Just then Mr. Woodpecker grabbed a bill full of suet, spread his wings, and flew to his favorite tree in the maple grove.

"Goody, goody, he's all better again," shouted Kathy, jumping up and down and clapping her hands.

"Oh, Mother, I'm glad you found him before Snowball did. It wasn't scary after we knew what made the noise."

KATHY'S PROBLEM

Kathy sighed.

Mother looked at her six-year-old helper. Kathy's usually sunny face was very sober, but she kept right on drying dishes.

"Mamma, what can I do when I am big?" she asked finally.

"Well," Mother said, smiling, "there are a lot of things you could do. What do you think you would like to do?"

"There are so many things to do, that I can't think which one I want to do most," answered Kathy. "You said you think Linda will make a good mamma because she takes such good care of the dolls. I think I would get tired of being a mamma. So, what can I do?"

Mother stooped down and smoothed a stray red curl from Kathy's cheek, then kissed her where the curl had been. "Before you were born, dear, God planned that Daddy and I should have a sweet, little baby girl. He planned that you should grow up to be Mamma's helper. That is what you are now. Helping Mother teaches and prepares you to do what God plans that you shall do when you are big."

"But, I would like to know now," said Kathy.

"Come, let's go out to the garden and plant some seeds," answered Mother. "I think we can learn something from the little seeds."

Linda quickly put Sally and Jane into their little, blue doll bed and covered them carefully with the pink blanket. "I want to go to the garden too," she said. "May I carry the seeds, please?"

Out to the garden the girls skipped while Mother walked more slowly. "Now what shall we plant?" she asked.

"Pumpkins for pumpkin pie," said Kathy, showing her dimples.

"Corn on the cob and red beets," added Linda, showing her dimples.

"All right, we will plant the red beets first," planned Mother.

"Oh, what funny little seeds! How can they grow into red beets?" asked Kathy. "They aren't red at all."

"No, they aren't red," agreed Mother. "But God planned that red beets should grow from these seeds, and He will make them grow."

Linda picked up the sweet corn seed. "This looks more like the corn we eat," she said.

Carefully the girls helped Mother drop the corn into the row. "This corn will grow taller than Mother's helpers before it forms the ears we will eat," explained Mother.

"Now we will put the pumpkins right here as far from the fence as we can," decided Mother. "If we put them too close to the fence, they will grow out into the field and the cows will eat them."

Kathy's brown eyes got even bigger. "How can they go that far?" she asked.

"That is the way God planned for them to grow," answered Mother. "The plant will have to grow and grow before there are any pumpkins. When it is a big plant, there will be yellow flowers. When a flower drops off, we will see a teeny little pumpkin. What color will it be when it is ready to make pies?"

"I know. I know," said Kathy. "It will be orange. My, my, how do those little seeds know what they are supposed to grow into—yellow corn, orange pumpkins, or red beets?"

"God makes them grow into the plant He has planned they should be," explained Mother. "Remember the Bible verse that tells us that when God made the world, He said every seed should yield after it's kind? He never lets a pumpkin grow on a cornstalk. It would break the plant down. He never lets corn grow on a pumpkin vine. It would rot if it were on the ground. Pumpkins have hard shells. It doesn't hurt them to lie on the ground."

"God must be very wise to do all that," said Kathy.

"Maybe when we go into the house we can make up a poem about God's wonders," suggested Mother.

Kathy loved poems. Her eyes sparkled. "Yes, let's go do it right now," she cried.

After the seeds were all carefully covered with soil, Mother, Kathy, and Linda went to the house.

Here is the poem they wrote:

The Seed's Secret

Tell me, little seed, how do you know
Into what tree or plant to grow?
A pretty flower or a lowly weed,
Who told you what to be, little seed?

One grows up, and we eat its fruits.
Another grows down, and we eat the roots.
From the butterfly seed
To the maple tree,
From the odd-shaped seed to the bright red
  beet.

Oh, 'tis not so hard to understand,
For God rules all with His mighty hand.
The all-wise Father who tells the seed what
  to be,
Will teach girls and boys like you and me.

Daddy was surprised when Mother read the poem in family worship that evening. Kathy snuggled against Mother and sighed. This time it was a happy sigh. "I'm not going to worry about what I will be when I am big," she said. "God will show me just as He shows the little seeds."

MOTHER'S DAY SURPRISE

Kathy tiptoed into the living room and quietly closed the door. She climbed up the back of Daddy's chair. "Daddy," she whispered. "What can Linda and I do for Mother on Mother's Day? Wayne and Larry made gifts for her in school, and we want to give her something too."

Daddy laid his book aside and drew Kathy into his strong arms. "Mother has an appointment with the dentist tomorrow," he whispered. "Maybe we can get something while Mother is at the dentist. Do you want to get some change out of your bank to buy something?"

Kathy's brown eyes sparkled, and she skipped back to the playroom to tell Linda and the boys her secret.

Linda ran to get her bank right away. Kathy,

Larry, and Wayne got their banks too, and ran upstairs. *Jingle, jangle, jingle!* What a noise the pennies, nickels, and dimes made as the children shook out their banks!

When Kathy awoke the next morning, she bounced right out of bed and dressed. Then she ran downstairs, "When is it time to go to the dentist?" she asked.

"My appointment is at ten-thirty," Mother answered. "That will give us time to do some cleaning before we go."

Three times after breakfast Kathy asked, "Is it time to go now?"

Finally Mother asked, "What makes you so anxious to get to the dentist, Kathy? Do you want to watch him fill my tooth?"

Kathy ran outside as though she hadn't heard Mother's question. Ten minutes later she was at the door again. "Is it time to go now?" she wanted to know.

Mother put the last blue barrette into Linda's pigtail and looked at the clock. "Just as soon as I get the tangles out of your curls, it will be time to get ready," she answered.

"Goody, goody," shouted Kathy and Linda. "May we wear our new green dresses?"

"Yes," Mother answered. "Get into them, and we will go."

Soon they were on the way to the dentist's office. When Daddy stopped the car, Mother said, "Who wants to go with me?" Nobody said a word. "What, no one wants to come with me? Daddy, can you keep tab of everyone and get all the things on this long list?" she asked.

"I think I can. If Linda holds onto my hand," Daddy said.

In a short time the children were following Daddy around the store as he bought thread, needles, ribbon, and the other things on Mother's list. But still they had no gift for Mother.

Just then Kathy saw the potted flowers. "Oh, let's get a flower. Mother loves flowers."

"Let's put all our money together and get one," said Wayne. "Larry and I made gifts in school, but we want to buy something too. We have a whole dollar."

"Yes, let's," agreed Kathy. "We won't find anything that Mother would like better than this flower."

All the children dropped their pennies, nickels, and dimes into Daddy's hand. Daddy counted them. "It's still not quite enough," he said. "But I want to help too. I will pay the rest."

Daddy counted more dimes out of his coin purse and gave them to the clerk. Wayne picked up the plant, and everyone went back to the car.

"How will we keep the plant hidden?" Wayne asked.

"Set it on the floor and put this box beside it. Now sit forward and keep your legs in front of it," suggested Daddy.

When they got to the dentist, Mother was ready to go. "We were in the store, Mamma,"

Linda began as soon as Mother came out to the car.

Kathy looked cross and squeezed Linda's arm to remind her to be quiet.

When they came home, Kathy almost forgot. "Who will bring the f . . . things in?" she asked.

Wayne shook his head and scowled. "I'll bring everything," he said.

Mother turned to the backseat. "Here, give me a load," she said. Wayne stretched his legs as big as he could in front of the flower, and Larry stuck his feet over to hide the pot. Would Mother see it? No, she took several packages and went to the house.

Quick as a wink, Wayne picked up the flower and dashed off to hide it in the basement.

The next morning before Mother and Father got up, Mother heard four pairs of feet softly tiptoeing about. "Now what wakened the children, and what are they doing?" she asked Daddy.

"Let's pretend to be asleep and see what they do," suggested Daddy.

Four pairs of brown eyes peeped in through a crack of the bedroom door. Quiet footsteps went pitter-patter down the stairs. Soon mysterious sounds of whispering, rattling plates, and clanging silverware came from downstairs. Next a delicious odor of toast drifted into the bedroom.

"Ummm, I'm getting hungry," said Mother.

"Me too," said Daddy. "Let's dress and wait till they call us."

Suddenly the door opened and four rosy-cheeked children chorused, "Happy Mother's Day."

"Thank you, children," Mother said, laughing.

"Come and see," said Linda. Taking Mother's hand, she led her down to the kitchen.

Breakfast was on the table. How good the orange juice and golden buttered toast looked. Around Mother's plate was a high wall of cereal boxes. Mother smiled, "Thank you, children. This is a fine surprise. You must think I am very hungry this morning," she laughed as she went to her place at the table.

Suddenly she stopped. "Oh, how beautiful. A lovely red azalea! Thank you. Thank you." Then she saw the two scratch pads the boys had made in school and the note tied to the flowers.

"To our mother because we love her," the note read. All their names were signed. Even Linda had printed hers with Daddy's help.

Mother smiled at everyone. "Thank you again," she said. "I feel like thanking God for a family who planned such a happy Mother's Day for me. Let's join hands and sing, 'I Thank the Lord My Maker.' "

LARRY'S MUMPS

Wayne pulled on his blue jeans and looked at Larry, still curled up under the bed covers. "Come on, slowpoke. Aren't you going along?" he asked.

Slowly Larry sat up on the edge of the bed and began pulling off his pajamas.

Wayne tied his last shoe and scooted down the stairs. "Hurry up or you'll be late," he called behind him.

"Ummm, ummm," he said, sniffing the steaming bacon and eggs waiting on the table.

Mother was pouring hot chocolate into the cups. "Where's Larry?" she asked.

"I don't know what ails him. He's only half awake. He isn't even dressed yet."

By and by Larry came slowly, slowly down the stairs. *Swish, swish,* his stocking feet dragged on the floor. *Plunk,* he threw his shoes down and slumped onto the couch.

Mother glanced at his flushed cheeks and

feverish eyes. "Don't you feel well?"

Larry didn't say a word. He just shook his head and blinked to hide the tears that wanted to spill from his big brown eyes.

Mother laid her cool hand on Larry's hot forehead. "I believe this boy needs the thermometer," she said.

Larry held the thermometer under his tongue for three minutes. Then Mother took it and looked at it. "Well," she said, "it says 101 degrees. You will stay at home today."

Larry began to sniffle. "Oh, Daddy, can't you wait till tomorrow to go to the city? I want to go along."

Daddy shook his head. "I am sorry, Larry, but the business must be taken care of today. I'll be going to the city again sometime when you can go along. Come eat your breakfast. Maybe you will feel better then."

Larry washed his face and slid into his place at the table. Daddy asked the blessing, and they began to eat.

But Larry just sat there. "Do I have to eat?" he asked. "It hurts under my ear when I swallow."

"Drink your orange juice if you don't feel like eating," suggested Mother.

Larry picked up his glass and took a sip of orange juice. He set it down so hard that some spilled. "Ouch! Oh, ouch! Oh that hurts," he cried. He screwed up his face and squirmed in his chair. Hot, salty tears rolled down his cheeks.

"Look at him," said Wayne. "His cheek is real fat. Just look. It's getting bigger."

Mother looked at Larry closely. Then she turned to Daddy. "Mumps! It must be mumps and the acid in the orange juice makes it hurt."

Larry didn't wait to be excused. He slipped away from the table and lay down on the couch. Mother brought him a white pill to swallow and a warm cloth to hold on his stinging jaw. After awhile he stopped crying.

When Daddy and Wayne said good-by, he began to sniffle again. "I wish I could go too."

"I'll read to you soon," Mother promised. Larry tried to smile, but because his cheek was so fat, the smile got crooked. Soon he grew drowsy and went back to sleep.

When Linda and Kathy came downstairs, Larry awoke. He was feeling better, but his cheeks were both so fat that Linda and Kathy laughed to see him. "He looks like a chipmunk with a nut in each cheek," Kathy said.

After the girls had their breakfast, Mother sat down and read to them till her throat was hoarse. Then Larry watched Kathy and Linda play dolls until Wayne and Daddy came home.

How Wayne laughed when he saw Larry's fat cheeks. "I'll bring you the mirror," he said, running to get it.

Larry did not think it was funny. He wanted to shout, "No!" But because his jaws ached, he only shook his head and turned his face to the wall.

Mother smiled. "Wait till your turn comes,

Wayne. Then Larry can bring the mirror to you."

"See what I brought for you," said Daddy, holding up *Yoni Wondernose* and *Sandy and Mr. Jalopy.* "These should entertain you for a while." Larry's eyes smiled, even though his face didn't look much like a smile.

For the next few days, Larry was quite sick. He could eat nothing but a few bites of ice cream, and drink some milk. Mother read *Yoni Wondernose* and *Sandy and Mr. Jalopy* to him. Larry laughed at funny parts of the stories, like when Ralph was a tomato at a program. Wayne brought a lot of old story papers from the attic and read those to him.

Then one day Larry felt well enough that he sat up in bed to play with pegs and put puzzles together. He was sure Mother should let him run and play.

"You must stay in bed," Mother insisted. "Remember, Dr. Stone said it is very important to stay in bed till all the swelling is gone."

"Staying in bed when you feel well is worse than being sick," Larry grumbled.

At last the day came when Larry could get into his clothes and run around again. "I'm glad I'm finished with the mumps," he sighed. "It wasn't much fun, but I did like the stories and the ice cream. And, Mother, you're good at taking care of mumpsy boys."

FAMILY SUNDAY

Kathy pushed her chair back from the breakfast table. "Mother, may Linda and I wear our new dresses today?" she asked.

Mother shook her head. "Did you forget? Larry is well again after having had the mumps, but we may be starting with mumps any time. So we can't go to Sunday school today."

Kathy's dimples disappeared, and her lower lip pushed out. "Not go to Sunday school," she wailed. "But, Mother, I don't want to miss Sunday school."

"I know, dear, and I'm sorry, but we might spread the mumps to a lot of people if we went to Sunday school today. How about packing our lunch and going to the pretty woods where I used to go after the cows when I was a girl?" Mother suggested. "We could have our own Sunday school under the trees."

"Yes! Yes!" shouted Wayne and Larry.

"May I take Sally Ann along?" asked Linda.

Mother smiled, "Yes, your dolly may go too," she promised.

Kathy frowned and blinked her big brown eyes to hide the tears that were shining there. "That won't seem like Sunday school at all," she protested.

"I think Sunday school in the woods will be nice," Daddy said. "We can learn a lot about God's world if we keep our eyes open."

"Okay then," Kathy agreed. "But I don't think I'll like Sunday school in the woods nearly as well as I do in church."

With everybody helping, the lunch was soon packed and they were on their way. Kathy's face was very sober when she saw her little friends going into the church as they passed. A little beyond the church, Daddy turned off onto a bumpy, dirt road. He stopped, and Wayne jumped out to open a big yellow gate.

Bump! Bump, bump, Daddy drove into a field where some red and white cows were grazing. *Bump! Bump, bump,* they went over rocks and bushes. Soon Daddy stopped the car. "We will have to walk the rest of the way," he said.

How cool and inviting the woods looked. Everybody scrambled out of the car and started down the hill to a big tree with a log under it.

Daddy sat down on the log and looked at his

watch. “It’s time for Sunday school to begin right now,” he said. Mother and the children sat down too.

“Let’s sing ‘Jesus Loves Me,’ ” said Linda. When the song was finished, Kathy wanted to sing “Father, We Thank Thee for the Night.” After that they bowed their heads while Daddy prayed. Then he read Psalm 24, and together they memorized the first two verses. Next Daddy taught the Sunday school lesson. Kathy’s dimples showed and her eyes sparkled. She hadn’t known Daddy was such a good teacher.

When the lesson was over, Daddy paused to watch a squirrel scamper down a tree and scold them for having a meeting under his home. “Shall we say the verses we learned again and sing a verse of ‘This is My Father’s World’? Then we can sit quietly and listen to God’s nature singing,” Daddy suggested. Mother and the children nodded in agreement.

After the song, everyone sat very still to be sure to hear everything. Kathy pushed her stray curls behind her ears so that she wouldn’t miss one sound. Suddenly a locust whirred and frightened Linda. Then a friendly phoebe bird peered out between some bushes and said, “Phoebe, phoebe,” as if to say, “What are you doing here?” Bobolinks called and a meadowlark sang his cheery song from a nearby field. A bright, red cardinal hopped from branch to branch of an evergreen. Then he spread his wings and flew away calling, "Good cheer, good cheer."

Then came the biggest surprise. A little gray bird settled in a bush and said, "Meow, meow, meow." Larry chuckled to hear a bird making cat sounds.

"It's a catbird. They are great imitators," Daddy explained. Daddy whistled like a bob-white.

"Bobwhite," echoed the catbird.

Daddy whistled, "Phoebe, phoebe, phoebe."

"Phoebe, phoebe, phoebe," answered the bird.

"Whippoorwill, whippoorwill," whistled Daddy.

"Whippoorwill," said the bird.

Larry forgot to be still. "Ha, ha, ha," he laughed.

And "Ha, ha, ha," said the catbird.

Larry's mouth fell open. "How does he do it?" Larry asked.

"God gave him the gift of imitating sounds," Daddy explained. Then he looked at his watch. "What, dinner time already?" he exclaimed.

After Mother put out the lunch, the family formed a circle and bowed their heads while Daddy asked the blessing.

Larry piled his plate with good things and put two fat ham sandwiches on top. "Umm, that looks good," he said. "Am I glad I can eat again! My plate's full now. I'll be back for my cherry pie later."

Mother, Daddy, Kathy, and Linda sat on a log to eat, while Wayne and Larry sat on a springy moss cushion.

When Kathy was finished eating, she leaned against Mother. "This was a fine day," she said. "I liked our Sunday school in the woods, the birds, the picnic, and just everything."

BUSHY TAIL'S NUTS

Linda put a green roof on the red brick house she was building. Suddenly she heard something. "Woo, woo," it went.

Linda's big brown eyes grew bigger. "What was that?" she asked.

"Oh, that was only North Wind howling," explained Kathy, who was a whole year older than Linda.

Linda walked over to the window to see. Just then the wind picked up a pile of leaves and blew them right at the window where Linda was standing.

Linda stepped back. "I don't like North Wind," she said. "He makes the pretty leaves come down, and he makes me shiver too."

By and by the wind stopped blowing, and the sun came out. "What a beautiful day!" said Mother, looking out the window. "If it warms up, we can gather nuts this afternoon."

After lunch Mother slipped a hot, juicy

cherry pie out of the oven. How good it smelled. Little red bubbles of juice were sputtering out of the round holes in the top.

"The pie is finished. Now who will help me pick up some hickory nuts in the pasture?" Mother asked.

"I will," said Linda with the brown pigtails.

"I will," said Kathy with the red pigtails.

"Fine," Mother smiled as she helped Linda into her rubbers, coat and hood. Kathy put on her rubbers and her blue coat and hood. Kathy and Linda got their sand buckets with pictures of Jack and Jill on the sides.

Mother got a big bucket with a picture of a black-and-white calf on the side.

Out the back door they all went. After climbing the fence, they walked through the pasture to the nut trees.

"Lots of nuts have fallen down, but they are covered with leaves. We will have to look hard to find them," Mother said.

Just then they heard something. "Chatter, chatter, chatter!" Everyone looked up. Away up at the top of the tree sat Bushy Tail, the little squirrel, scolding with all his might.

"He thinks we are taking his nuts," Mother explained.

"Are they his nuts?" Kathy asked in surprise. "We shouldn't take his nuts, should we, Mother?"

Mother smiled. "There are more nuts than he can eat. So it will be all right for us to take some."

Bushy Tail ran up and down the tree, and how he did scold! Linda put a nut right at the foot of the tree. Bushy Tail grabbed it with his mouth. How funny he looked with the nut in his cheek.

"He looks like Larry did when he had the mumps," Kathy said, laughing.

Bushy Tail hurried up the tree with his nut and popped into the hole that was his home. In a minute he came back down and scolded some more. Kathy threw a nut at him, and Bushy Tail scurried away. Very soon he returned, grabbed the nut, and ran away toward another tree.

There he stopped and scratched with his front feet so that the leaves flew up over his tail. Then he dropped the nut into the hole he had dug and covered it up. How the girls laughed.

"Why did he do that?" Linda wanted to know.

"I know," Kathy answered. "He buried the nut to eat this winter. But how does he know he should do that?" she wondered.

"God lets the animals know how to take care of themselves," Mother explained. "We say He gave them the instinct to store food for winter. Bushy Tail does not have hands to prepare things for canning, so he buries his food."

Kathy's and Linda's cheeks grew rosy from the cool November air. Soon the buckets were all filled. Then they sat down on a log to take the thick, green shells off the nuts.

Presently Bushy Tail came rushing down the tree and grabbed another nut. Back he raced up the tree to his home. Soon he was returning for another nut. Again and again he found nuts.

"How can he find so many nuts? I thought we picked up the last ones," said Kathy.

"Well," began Mother, "God gave him very good eyes to find them. That is one way He helps the animals find food. And Bushy Tail can smell nuts too. So he can find them better than we can."

"But how can he crack them without a hammer?" Linda wanted to know.

Mother smiled. "God gave squirrels very sharp, strong teeth with which to crack nuts," she said.

Linda looked thoughtful, then sighed happily. "God surely knows how to take care of the animals. And I guess North Wind is all right too. He brings the nuts down where Bushy Tail and we can both get them."

Wayne and Larry came home on the school bus just as Mother and the girls were going to the house. They came over and held the fence wire up so that Mother could get through easier, and then they all walked to the house together.

WHO GOT THE NUTS?

"Bushy Tail must have been very busy. This is all the nuts we could find this time," said Wayne as he set the bucket of hickory nuts on the kitchen floor.

"Thank you," said Mother. "You may take them right up to the attic and put them into the box with the other nuts."

Wayne clumped up the stairway and crossed the hall to the attic door. Then he climbed the narrow attic stairway to the top.

"Mother! Mother!" he called. "Someone has been taking our nuts. There are only a few in the box anymore."

Mother hurried to the door. "What?" she asked. "Are you sure you are looking in the right box?"

"Yes, I'm sure," Wayne answered. His voice sounded muffled from high in the attic.

Mother clumped up the steps too. Chubby Larry, pigtailed Linda, and red-haired Kathy followed. Sure enough, the box was nearly empty.

"Now, who do you suppose took all those nuts that we wanted for Christmas candies?" Wayne asked.

"Do you think it was a robber?" Larry wanted to know.

Mother smiled. "I don't think a robber would bother with a few nuts."

"Well, who took them then?" Wayne asked. "Maybe Bushy Tail found his way up here and took our nuts for his own. I know—I'll get the box trap I made for opossums and catch him if he's the thief."

Wayne got the trap and tied a nut to the tripper for bait. Mother put the rest of the nuts into a bucket and covered them so that no animal could get them. Then everyone went downstairs.

After supper, Wayne went upstairs to look at his trap. The nut was gone, but there was no sign of Bushy Tail in the trap. *How did he get that nut out without getting caught?* Wayne wondered. He put screen over the end of the trap, put another nut on the tripper, and went to bed.

The next morning the nut was gone again, but the trap was empty.

"It looks to me as though a mouse is taking the nuts," said Daddy.

"Oh, a mouse couldn't carry so many nuts away," Wayne disagreed. But he ran downstairs to ask Mother for some flour to spread on the floor so that they could see what tracks the animal made.

After school Wayne looked at the tracks. "Mother," he called. "There are lots of tiny tracks around here. I don't know if they are squirrel tracks or not."

Mother clumped upstairs and looked closely. "I do believe they are mouse tracks," she decided.

"I'll play a trick on that mouse," planned Wayne. "I'll tie a long string to a nut, then we can follow the string and find the place where she hid the nuts." And he did just that. But do you think the little mouse showed him where the nuts were? No, it didn't. The mouse snipped off the string with its sharp little teeth and ran away with the nut while Wayne was sleeping.

"She's really a smart one," laughed Wayne when he saw the snipped string. "But I'll trick her. I'll fasten some thin wire to the nut. She can't bite that off."

And he did. But do you think that little mouse showed him where the nuts were? No, she didn't. The mouse nibbled and nibbled till it cut through the shell of the nut and ate it right there while Wayne was in school.

"I will get her this time," said Wayne. He ran downstairs and got a mousetrap. Mother gave him some yellow cheese to put on the trap for bait. It smelled so good that Wayne took a bite. Then he took the trap, set it, and put it down right beside the box trap.

That night Mrs. Mouse went to see if she could find a nut. She smelled something delicious. Could it be cheese way up here in the attic? It was. She took a big bite. Snap! The trap went off before she could swallow it. Wayne found her the next morning.

"Poor, poor mouse, you were a smart one, but you let some cheese tempt you. So I got you at last." He picked up the trap and went down to show the mouse to the family.

Linda and Kathy climbed onto chairs behind the table.

Wayne laughed. "She won't hurt you. She's dead." He held up the trap so that everyone could see the mouse. The fur on its back was a soft velvety gray. Underneath it was white and soft as cotton.

"Look at her long, skinny tail," said Kathy.

"See these tiny feet. They work like shovels. And her beady black eyes can see in the dark," Daddy explained.

"What are mice for?" Larry wanted to know.

"This is a white-footed deer mouse," said Daddy. "They usually stay in fields where they eat lots of weed seeds and insects. But I suppose this one wanted to find a warm place for winter."

"He found a good place . . . and some food, too, only it was ours," said Larry.

LARRY'S PAINTED TOES

Chubby Larry came back to the picnic table the third time. This time he took pie, potato chips, and cookies. "I wish I could eat more," he said.

"Come on, let's get back to playing," said James, his best chum, who couldn't manage a third helping.

"All right," said Larry, stuffing the last bite of cookie into his mouth. Away they ran to join a group of boys under a tree.

"Let's play follow-the-leader," suggested Larry, wiggling his toes in delight as he ran through the soft green moss. "This moss really feels good to bare feet," he said.

All the boys took off their shoes and piled them behind a log.

"We're ready," said the boys. "You be the leader, Larry."

Larry jumped up onto a stump. Swinging his arms, he took a big jump. Down he went into the tall grass below.

"Ouch! Oh, ouch!" he cried, standing on one foot. "I stepped into something." Blood was trickling from his foot.

"You better find your mother quick. It's really bleeding," said Jack.

Larry hobbled away to find Mother. James ran ahead to tell her Larry had been hurt.

"What happened?" asked Mother, coming to meet him. She set Larry down on the grass and looked at his foot. Daddy brought the first-aid kit from the car. He put some powder on the cut and helped Mother bandage it to stop the bleeding.

All the boys and girls and lots of people crowded around to see what had happened. "Does it hurt?" they wanted to know.

"Of course it hurts," said Larry blinking his brown eyes.

"It's a pretty bad cut," said Daddy to Mother. "Do you think I had better take him to the doctor?"

"Yes, I think you should," agreed Mother. "I will get our things together. We will be ready to go home when you get back."

Daddy sat down and told Larry to climb onto his back. "Oh, my," he grunted when he got up. "Such a chubby boy, and with all that picnic dinner you ate, no wonder you're heavy." Then he carried Larry to the car.

"What will the doctor do?" Larry asked nervously.

"I don't know just what he will do,"

answered Daddy. "He may only put a clean bandage on your foot, or he may have to stitch it up so that it can heal properly."

Larry's eyes got big and round. "That will hurt," he said. "I don't want to go to the doctor. It doesn't hurt now anymore."

"I will stay right with you, and the doctor will be very careful," Daddy said. "Someone else will be with you too. The Bible says, 'He is a present help in time of trouble.' Shall we ask Him to help you to be brave?"

Larry nodded.

"Dear God," prayed Daddy, "help Larry be brave and trust You to be with him in his trouble. Amen."

Daddy drove as fast as he dared. Soon Larry was riding Daddy's back into Dr. Smith's waiting room.

"Bring him right into the office," said Nurse Thompson when she saw the bloody bandage.

Daddy stood right beside Larry while the doctor carefully removed the bandage Mother had put on his foot. "I'll have to do some cleaning, so that I can get a good look at the cut," explained Doctor Smith. He dipped some cotton into alcohol and began to clean.

Larry squirmed, but he didn't jerk his foot back. He held as still as he possibly could. "I'll have to put in a few stitches for it to heal up right," said Doctor Smith when he had finished cleaning.

With a swab of cotton, Nurse Thompson painted antiseptic all around the cut.

"Now, Larry," said the doctor, showing him a small syringe. "This will sting a bit. But it will numb your foot so that the stitching will not hurt you."

Larry held Daddy's hand tightly and remembered that God was with him too.

"There, that's all you will feel," said Doctor Smith. "You certainly are a brave boy. I thought Miss Thompson and your daddy would have to hold you down while I did that. Now I'm going to sew you up with purple thread."

Larry grinned. "It just tickles," he whispered to Daddy.

"Will you hand me the purple paint, please, Miss Thompson?" asked Doctor Smith when the last stitch was in. "I'll put this on the wound to help it heal." Then he winked at Daddy and began to paint all the toes bright purple. "These toes should be painted so that no one will step on them," he said.

Larry laughed. He knew Doctor Smith was just being funny.

"We must keep his foot clean," explained Doctor Smith. He began to wrap white gauze around and around until Larry's foot was great big and only the purple toes stuck out.

"Now, there is one more thing I must do," the doctor said. "Larry needs a shot to safeguard against tetanus."

Larry's face grew sober, but he pulled up his sleeve and held out his chubby arm for the shot. Did he cry? No indeed, and just as soon as it was over, he smiled such a big smile that all his dimples showed.

Turning to his desk, Doctor Smith opened the top drawer. Larry peeped in. There were red, yellow, green, brown, orange, and purple suckers in it.

"Pick two," said Doctor Smith. "You were a good boy and deserve two lollipops."

Larry's brown eyes sparkled. "I'll take a purple one to match my toes," he grinned. "Thank you, Doctor."

Doctor Smith smiled a big, friendly smile. "You're welcome, sonny. I wish all my little patients were as good as you were."

On the way home, Larry took the sucker out of his mouth long enough to say, "Doctor Smith sure is a nice doctor. And God did help me be brave and trust Him."

Daddy looked over at Larry and smiled.

SECTION TWO

PEGGY VISITS BUTTONVILLE

Peggy gave her pillow such a hard thump that it sailed right off her bed down onto the floor. "I don't like this old bed," she said. "It isn't fair that I have been sick and have to stay in bed when Jack and Patty can be outside."

Mother picked up the pillow and put it back onto the bed. "Why not play with some of the nice things that were in your sunshine box?" she suggested.

"No," Peggy answered. "Those things aren't nice. I'm tired of playing with them. I wish I had something new."

"Well, how about stirring up a cake for me with the little mixer Uncle Paul sent and baking it in the pans from Aunt Hazel?"

Peggy shook her head and dabbed at a tear in the corner of one blue eye. "No! I want to go outside. I don't see why I have to stay in bed. Besides, I asked God to make Dr. Glass say I could get up today. Why didn't He answer my prayer, Mother?"

Mother sat on the edge of the bed. She took Peggy's small white hand in her strong brown one. "Peggy dear, does Daddy always say yes when you ask him for something?" she asked.

Peggy thought for a minute. "No . . . not always," she admitted.

"And don't you think it's the same with your heavenly Father?" suggested Mother. "Sometimes He has to say no too. Maybe God wants to teach you some lesson before you get well, like being happy wherever you are."

Peggy frowned and gave her pillow another thump. "I don't see how anyone could be happy in bed," she said.

Mother sighed. "Let's ask God to help us think of ways to keep you happy."

Peggy looked doubtful, but she listened quietly with bowed head and closed eyes while Mother prayed. Then Mother said, "You are tired from your trip to the doctor this morning. You can help answer the prayer by taking a nice rest while I do the dishes."

How can I help answer a prayer? she wondered. But she snuggled down to rest, covering her face with one arm like a chicken hiding its head when it goes to sleep. Only she was hiding the tears that kept slipping down her cheeks.

When the dishes were finished, Mother tiptoed into Peggy's bedroom. Peggy was fast asleep. Mother gently brushed back Peggy's damp, blonde hair, smoothed the bed, and quietly left the room.

Later on Jack came in with the afternoon mail. "Here's a parcel. May I open it?" he asked.

"Yes, open it," Mother replied. "I think it's only buttons for the sewing circle."

"Buttons, buttons, and more buttons; you are right, Mother," he said.

Mother took the buttons and started to the sewing cupboard. But then she thought of something. She went to the kitchen and dumped all the buttons into a big cake pan. Then returning to Peggy's room, she set Sally Jo, Peggy's favorite doll, on the bed with Peggy. Then she printed some letters on a piece of paper and tied the paper to Sally Jo's arm. She set the pan of buttons on Sally Jo's lap and arranged some things on the table by Peggy's bed. Then she hurried off to work.

By and by Peggy opened one blue eye and yawned. She stretched a big stretch and opened both blue eyes. "Moth . . . ," she began in a whiny voice. Then she saw Sally Jo sitting against the wall with the note on her arm. Peggy sat up straight. She saw the buttons. "Mother," she called excitedly. "What does this note say?"

Mother hurried into the bedroom. "It says, 'Welcome to Buttonville,' Peggy."

Peggy stared. Then she began to smile. On the table was the pretty rose tea set her

Sunday school class had given her, the toy mixer, the baking set, and the little iron stove that was Mother's when she was a little girl. All the other dolls were sitting on chairs looking as though they were expecting something. Peggy smiled a big smile and began to stir the buttons with a spoon from the baking set.

Just then Patty came into the house. "Oh, my! It's warm out there," she said, tossing back her brown pigtails and wiping her damp face. "I'm going to stay inside and play with Peggy."

"Let's cook a big dinner and invite all the dolls," Peggy planned. She filled a tiny kettle with green button peas, another one with white button potatoes, and the frying pan with brown button steak. Patty set them all on the little, old cookstove to cook.

"I will bake a cake," said Patty.

"I will read the recipe for you," Peggy said, reaching for the little cookbook. Patty got the tiny measuring cup. "Six cups of sugar," Peggy said, pretending to read.

Patty put six tin cups of white button sugar into the mixing bowl. "Two cups butter, seven eggs," read Peggy. In went yellow buttons. "Five cups flour and one cup milk," read Peggy. Patty put in lots of white buttons. "That's all," said Peggy.

Patty pressed the little knob on the mixer. Z-z-z-zip, the little mixer started. Buttons flew in all directions, as popcorn did when Mother let the lid come off the popper. How the girls laughed! Patty laughed until she sat right down on the floor with the buttons and began picking them up. Jack, who had just come into the house, laughed too, and got down on the floor to help her. At last the cake was finished.

When everything was ready, Patty set the table, and all the dolls came to the big dinner. Patty filled each plate with colorful buttons. Peggy said grace and began to feed the dolls.

Suddenly Patty began to choke, and cough. "Whaa," she cried. Mother hurried to the playroom to see what was the matter.

Peggy and Patty and Jack laughed and laughed! "That was only Sally Jo choking on her cookie," Peggy explained.

Mother laughed too, and returned to the kitchen. By and by, she came in with a soft, green washcloth, pink soap, and warm water. "Time to wash up for supper," she smiled.

Peggy looked surprised. "Supper time already?" she asked. "Oh, Mother, God really helped you think of something to make me happy. I think I'll go to Buttonville every day until I get out of bed."

Mother stooped and kissed Peggy's clean, upturned face. "And you helped answer the prayer by resting so that you felt better."

Peggy sighed a happy little sigh. "And Patty helped too. She came in to play with me."

TOMMY GOES BACK TO SCHOOL

"When does school begin?" asked Tommy.

Mother glanced at the calendar. "Two weeks from today," she answered.

Tommy frowned. "Oh, no! I don't want to go to school this year. I'd rather stay home and run after Daddy and ride on the tractor with him."

"But think of all the things you learned and all the good times you had last year," Mother reminded him.

"Oh, yes, I know I learned a lot," answered Tommy. "I think I know all I need to know now. I can read and print. I can do problems, and I can spell words. So why should I go to school?"

Mother smiled. "Well, that is fine," she said. "If you can do all that, you can finish filling out this order while I do the dishes. Then we can both go to the garden and pick those speckled, bird-egg beans."

"All right," agreed Tommy. "What shall I order?"

"Everything is on the order sheet except these three shirts," answered Mother, showing him which ones. "Write this number right here. Put a three in this little box. Write *shirts* on this line, *size eight* here, and *blue* here. Put the price and the postage in the column as it tells you."

Mother went to do the dishes, and Tommy got to work. It took a long time to print the numbers and words on those little lines.

"Mother," he called, "how do I know what three shirts cost?"

"Multiply by three," answered Mother.

Tommy's brown eyes grew big. "But I don't know how to do that," he said.

Mother smiled as she helped him. "Now you will need to add this long column of numbers to get the total," she explained. "When you are finished with that, I will show you how to add postage and tax."

Mother went back to the dishes, and Tommy's brown head bent over the order sheet. How he did work. But there were so many numbers he got all mixed up.

"Mother," he called again as though he were ready to cry. "How can I add all these numbers? I get all mixed up."

"Well," said Mother, "maybe there is something for you to learn in school after all."

Tommy looked at the floor. "I guess you're right," he said. "I can do problems, but not such big ones. I suppose if I want to be Daddy's helper when I grow up, I'd better go to school and learn to do big problems too."

On a Tuesday morning in September, Tommy put on one of the blue shirts he had helped to order. For breakfast Tommy had cold orange juice, warm toast, an egg, and cereal that crackled when he added milk.

After breakfast he helped Mother pack his lunch. He slipped two of Mother's good chocolate chip cookies into a sandwich bag and put them into his lunch box. Then he snapped the lid shut. Suddenly he thought of something. "Mother," he said, "may I take a cookie along for Miss Burkey?"

"Certainly, you may," said Mother. "That will be a good way to get acquainted with your new teacher."

Quickly he opened the lunch box again and put in another cookie. Then he ran outside to wait for the bus. He looked both ways before crossing the highway.

"Good morning," said Bobby, Peter, and Jack when he climbed into the bus. He hadn't seen Peter since school closed last spring.

At the schoolhouse, more friends greeted him. "Hi, Tommy," said Arthur, his best chum. "Say, it's great to see you again. Let's choose sides and play ball."

What fun they had playing ball, but soon the bell rang. Tommy wished they could keep playing. But inside, the schoolroom was nice and cool. The windows were open, and he could hear his favorite robins and bluebirds singing.

How nice this is! he thought. *It smells so fresh and clean. I think I'll learn a lot this year.*

Miss Burkey smiled at Tommy as she thanked him for the cookie. "I am sure we are going to have fine times this school term," she said.

When Tommy came home from school, he hurried into the house, letting the screen door bang behind him. "Mother," he called. "We had a great time in school. Miss Burkey is such a nice teacher, and the schoolroom was so pretty. I think I'll learn lots and lots this year."

"That's fine," said Mother. "I was sure you would like school."

Tommy remembered to say a special "thank you" for school when he said his prayer that evening.

WHERE IS RICHARD?

Richard, Shirley, and Rodney were helping Daddy and Mother at the sugar camp. Daddy took the sap pails off the storage rack, and the children carried them over to Mother who was washing them. Back and forth, back and forth they trudged. Richard's chubby arms and legs grew tired.

"There, those are the last ones," Daddy said finally. Turning to the children, he added, "You have been good helpers. Now you may play while Mother and I finish the sap pails."

"Goody, goody!" cheered Rodney. "Let's play hide-and-seek."

"Yes, let's," agreed Shirley, remembering all the good places to hide around the sugar camp.

What fun the children had! Sometimes they hid inside the camp among the sap pails and stacks of wood. Sometimes they hid outside behind trees, the sugar-water wagon, the tractor, or the woodpile.

When Shirley was *it,* she soon found Rodney and began to look for Richard. She looked and looked. Rodney helped. They looked inside and outside the camp, here, there, everywhere they thought a little boy could hide. But Richard was not to be found. They called and called. There was no answer.

"I wonder if Richard sneaked over to the Yommers'," Shirley said.

"We'll go right over and see," declared Rodney. So off went the children through the deep snow, around trees, over bumps, and across the lane to the Yommers' house.

Mrs. Yommer's blue eyes opened wide in surprise when she saw Rodney and Shirley on her porch. "Is Richard hiding here?" asked Rodney. "We were playing hide-and-seek, and we can't find him."

"No, I haven't seen Richard," she said, dusting the flour off her hands. "Did you children walk up here by yourselves?"

"We walked from the sugar camp," Rodney explained. "We were helping Mother and Daddy wash sap pails. Then we played hide-and-seek."

"Well," said Mrs. Yommer thoughtfully, "Richard has not been here. You had better go back and tell your mother and daddy you cannot find him. But come in and warm up a bit first. There's a cold wind starting to blow."

The children stepped inside the warm kitchen. The delicious smell of chocolate cookies rushed toward them. Mrs. Yommer hurried to the oven to rescue the last panful. While the children warmed up, she brought them each two fat cookies, shook the snow out of Shirley's boots, and found a pair of dry mittens for Rodney. Then, warm and cozy, they set out for the sugar camp.

Meanwhile, Mother washed the last sap pail and stood up to rest her tired back. "It seems a long time since the children were in here," she said. "I wonder where they are."

Daddy rinsed the last sap pail and added it to the stack waiting to go out to the maple trees. "It does seem a long time," he agreed. "We had better go and check on them."

Daddy and Mother went outside. The children were not in sight. "Rodney! Shirley! Richard!" they called over and over. There was no answer. Daddy walked up the lane and looked around. "Here are tracks through the groves toward Yommers'."

Mother's brown eyes looked worried. "Come, let's go look for them."

Quickly they got into the car and started out the lane. The wind had begun to blow, and sharp pellets of snow bounced on the windshield.

While Mother and Daddy started off in the car, the children were coming back through the wind and snow toward the sugar camp. The sharp little pellets smarted in the children's faces. Their cheeks grew red and cold. Shirley began to cry. When Daddy and

Mother came to the top of the hill, they saw the children coming.

Daddy stopped the car. "What's wrong? Where have you been?"

Rodney burst into tears, "We . . . we . . . can't find Richard," he sobbed. "We were playing hide-and-seek, and he got lost. We called and called, and we looked at Yommers'. Richard just isn't anywhere!"

Jumping out of the car, Daddy and Mother hugged the children and brushed the snow off their clothes. "Well, well, you really tried," Daddy said, "but you should have told Mother and me that you couldn't find Richard." Then he added, "Let's ask Jesus to help us find him."

They all bowed their heads, and Daddy prayed. "Dear Jesus, please help us find Richard. Rodney and Shirley have tried to find him, but we need Your help. Thank you, Jesus. Amen."

"Maybe Richard decided to go home," Mother suggested. "Jump into the car, and we will look there first of all."

Daddy opened the back door, and the children climbed in. Too tired to pull the blanket off the seat, they plunked down onto it. Ooops! Something soft and bumpy was under the blanket. Rodney jerked it off. And guess what? There was Richard fast asleep!

"Goody, goody!" shouted Shirley.

"God answered our prayer quickly," added Rodney.

Richard sat up, rubbing his big brown eyes. Then remembering that he had been playing hide-and-seek, he scrambled to his feet. "Free, free!" he shouted.

AUTUMN HELPERS

Rodney scooted to the edge of his chair. He wanted to hear all about the Autumn Project his Sunday school teacher was planning for the primary class.

"How many of you boys and girls know the elderly couple living on Chestnut Street?" Sister Eby asked.

Most of the children raised their hands. But Rodney wasn't sure. "Do you mean the old John Millers?" he asked.

"That's right," answered Sister Eby. "You've probably noticed the tree in their backyard?"

Rodney nodded. He was thinking of the times he'd wished for one of those pears on his way home from school.

"Well, Mr. Miller fell off a ladder when he was picking pears and hurt his ankle," said Mrs. Eby. "Mrs. Miller has rheumatism and can't get around very well. They need some help."

Rodney slumped back in his chair. "I'm

not interested in helping those grouchy old people," he said to himself.

"I was thinking," Sister Eby continued, "that you boys and girls might like to help Mr. Eby and me pick pears, gather nuts, and clean up their yard for them. How many of you think you could help?"

"I think I can," said Shirley and Linda in one breath.

"We'll bring our wheelbarrow to haul leaves," offered Jack and James.

"I'll bring my wagon," added Bobby.

"And we'll bring buckets to pick up nuts," said Jane and Peggy.

Sister Eby looked at Rodney expectantly, but he didn't say a word. A puzzled look crossed her face. "That will be fine," she said. "All those who can help, please meet us at Millers' tomorrow after school. We will be real autumn helpers."

On the way home, Rodney told Mother and Daddy about the plan. "But I'm not going," he said.

"Not going?" Daddy asked in surprise. "Why, I think it's a good idea. You won't only be helping the Millers, but you'll have fun and get acquainted with your teacher and pastor."

Rodney shrugged his shoulders. "Maybe so, but I don't want to help that stingy old man. He won't even look at me when I say 'Hi' to him on my way home from school. I think he's afraid I might take one of his old pears. Besides, I have other plans."

On Monday the boys and girls in Sister Eby's class hurried home from school, that is, all except Rodney. He just shuffled along. When he met Bobby already on his way to the Millers' with his red wagon, he frowned. "Who will I play with?" he asked himself.

"Come along, you'll be late," Bobby called as he zoomed past.

For a minute Rodney stared after him. Then he pulled his blue cap down tight and dashed toward home. "Mother," he shouted, "I'm going to the Millers' after all. May I take our rake along?"

Mother looked up from the apples she was paring. "You surely may." She smiled. "Have a nice time."

Rodney got the rake and hurried to the Millers' backyard.

"Well, here comes Rodney," exclaimed Sister Eby with a smile. "Very good! Now we have perfect attendance for the Autumn Project. Let's get started."

"All right," said Brother Eby, climbing the ladder and picking pears into a bucket. Rodney looked up at him. It seemed funny to see the pastor up in a tree, but he knew how to pick all right. There was no question about that.

The girls helped Sister Eby gather nuts. A saucy red squirrel raced up and down the tree, scolding loudly. But the girls kept on picking up nuts and only laughed at his nut-filled cheeks.

The boys raked up huge piles of leaves and loaded them onto the wagon and the wheelbarrow. James crawled onto the wheelbarrow to press down the leaves, and Jack drove off toward the garden. When the wheelbarrow hit a bump, over it went. Down tumbled James with leaves falling all over him. How everybody laughed! For a while the boys forgot about working and rolled in the leaves, trying to cover each other up. Even Brother Eby climbed down from his perch in the pear tree and joined in the fun.

Soon they went back to work. They kept on until the yard was cleared of leaves and all the nuts were picked up. The leaves were dumped at the far end of the garden and weighted down so they wouldn't blow away. The baskets of pears were placed in the pantry.

Mrs. Miller stood at the window, her face wreathed in smiles, and her gray eyes sparkling. Just as the group was ready to leave, she opened the window and called them all inside.

"Come in, come in," called Mr. Miller from his rocking chair. His swollen ankle was wrapped in bandages and resting on a low stool. The children could smell liniment. Rodney was surprised to see a friendly twinkle in the old man's eyes. And he noticed that, even though Mr. Miller was wearing hearing aids, it was hard for him to understand. *So that's why he never looks up when I say "Hi" to him,* Rodney thought.

While Mr. Miller was welcoming them, Mrs. Miller limped from the kitchen with plates heaped with popcorn and homemade cookies and candies. Nestled in the center of the popcorn were cups of hot chocolate with pumpkin marshmallows floating on top. Rodney's blue eyes sparkled. He thought he had never tasted anything so good.

Everybody chatted happily while they ate. Then Brother Eby stood up. "Thank you for the delicious snack," he said. "Now we really must be going."

"You're welcome," exclaimed Mrs. Miller. "And thank you for all you've done." She passed a plump paper bag to each one, and added, "We can't tell you what it means to us. But here's a little something to show our appreciation."

Outside it was growing dark, and the moon was already peeping above the mountain. Rodney got his rake and hurried home. "Mother, Daddy," he said as he burst into the kitchen, "we really had fun. The Millers are nice old folks. Mr. Miller is hard-of-hearing, but he really loves children."

Opening his bag, Rodney peeped inside. His cheeks burned as he showed Daddy and Mother the pears inside. "And to think that I blamed Mr. Miller for being too stingy to give me a pear," he stammered. "They gave each of us a bag like this."

Daddy smiled. "There's something nice about most people if you look for it."

GOOD-BY HEADACHE

Randy, Millard, and Brian bounced off the school bus and raced down the alley. "Let's meet at the vacant lot at five o'clock and play ball," Randy suggested.

"Okay, suits me fine," answered Brian. "I need lots of practice."

"Me too," agreed Millard. The three boys skipped along merrily.

Just as Randy turned in at the Bender drive, he saw his mother in the garden. Suddenly his feet seemed to get heavy. "Oh, bother," he mumbled. "Mother wants me to help her in the garden this evening."

By the time he had reached the house, he felt so sorry for himself that he could almost feel a little pain on the left side of his head.

"Run on in and change clothes right away, then come out and help me," Mother called.

Randy's feet dragged as he went upstairs. He wiggled out of his school pants and into his old, brown corduroy trousers and a patched shirt. He got his blue jacket and trudged out to the garden. Flopping down on his red wagon, he propped his head in his hands and squinted his blue eyes up at Mother. "Do I have to help? My . . . my head sort of hurts," he stammered.

Mother looked up sharply. "Headache again?" she asked. "You sounded fine when you were coming down the alley with the other boys. But, of course, I won't insist that you help if you aren't feeling well. Go on upstairs and lie down. Sally will soon be waking up, and I'll have to come in. Then I'll bring you something to make you feel better."

Randy's cheeks burned as he trudged toward the house. *Did Mother hear our plans about playing ball?* he wondered. Slowly he crept upstairs and stretched out on the bed. *Maybe if I rest awhile I can convince her I'm all right and she will let me go to the vacant lot,* he thought.

After a while he heard Mother come inside and walk around in the kitchen. Soon she came upstairs carrying a tray loaded with a cup of hot tea, a glass of water, and a glass of orange juice. "Your frequent headaches puzzle me," she said seriously. "I'm going to try Grandma's herb tea. If it doesn't help, you'll have to see the doctor."

Mother handed Randy the steaming cup. "It's a mixture Grandma used on us when we were ailing. Drink it, and you can probably say good-by to your headache."

Randy took a little sip. Then he sputtered,

coughed, and gagged. "Horrid!" he exploded.

"I know it's bitter," she sympathized. "But you've got to take it. Hold your breath and drink it as fast as you can."

Randy took a deep breath and gulped the mixture down. Then he grabbed the water and swallowed it without stopping. Then he grabbed the orange juice and drank most of it to get rid of the bitter taste. "That taste is terrible enough to cure anything," he exclaimed.

"Now lie down and take a nap," Mother instructed. "Aunt Betty tells me the measles have been in school. Maybe you're coming down with measles." Just then Sally began crying, and Mother hurried downstairs.

At five-fifteen, Randy heard Brian and Millard talking to Mother.

"Isn't Randy coming to the vacant lot to play ball?"

"Coming to the vacant lot?" Mother said in surprise. "No, he's complaining of headache. He can't come."

"Maybe he's better now," they suggested.

Randy was just ready to call out that he was all right when he heard Mother say firmly, "No, I gave him some medicine, and he can't go out."

Randy could hear Mother and Sally talking. The delicious smell of baking apple dumplings drifted upstairs. He was beginning to feel a little lonely.

Soon Mother brought him a bowl of bread and milk. "This is all you can have after a dose of Grandma's "Good-by Headache Tea," she explained.

During supper, Mother told Daddy about Randy's frequent headaches and the cure she was trying. Randy heard Daddy laugh, but he didn't hear him say, "I doubt whether he will need to see the doctor."

Later in the evening, Randy heard a car drive in. Daddy's deep voice reached Randy upstairs. "Well, well, what a pleasant surprise. Hello Jim, Ella, George, Marvin. Hi, Susie! Come on in, everybody."

Randy scooted out of bed and slid out to the stairway where he could see and hear.

"Where's Randy?" asked his cousins, George and Marvin.

"He was complaining of headache. I gave him some of Grandma's herb tea and sent him to bed," Mother explained.

"I feel all right now. Can't I come down and play with the boys, please?" Randy called down the stairs.

Mother glanced up at him. "I'm sorry, Randy, but we can't take any chances. If you would be coming down with the measles, little Susan might catch them. You'll have to go back to your room and stay there."

Randy dragged himself back to his room and slumped down on the bed. "Oh, if only I hadn't told Mother I had a headache, then I wouldn't be missing out on all this fun," he chided himself. Then he remembered Brother Weaver's sermon. Brother Weaver had said lying was sin and liars would be punished. Big tears rolled down over Randy's flushed cheeks and landed on his green blanket.

After Uncle Jims were gone, Mother slipped upstairs to check on Randy. She saw the trace of tears on his face. "I'm sorry you couldn't play with Marvin and George, Randy," she said sympathetically. "They were disappointed too."

Randy buried his face in his pillow and sobbed. "It's my fault, Mother. I didn't really have a headache. I just didn't want to help you in the garden. I'm sorry, Mother. Please forgive me."

Mother sat down on the edge of the bed and drew Randy close. "Sure, I'll forgive you," she comforted him.

Randy clung to Mother, still sobbing. "Di . . . did . . . didn't Brother Weaver say that liars will be punished?" he asked.

"That's right," Mother answered, "if they do not repent and stop lying. But if you are sorry and ask God to forgive you, He is always ready to forgive. Would you like to ask God to forgive you now?"

Randy scrambled out of bed and knelt beside Mother. "Dear Jesus," he prayed. "I am sorry I told Mother I had a headache when I really didn't. Please forgive me and help me to always be truthful. Amen." Then he jumped back into bed.

Ten minutes later, Mother looked into Randy's room. He was fast asleep with a smile on his face.

GLENN'S FUN WAGON

Glenn tossed back the covers and bounced out of bed. "Today is my birthday," he told himself as he dived into his jeans and plaid shirt. The aroma of scrambled eggs and toast greeted him as he scooted down the stairs.

"Happy birthday!" said Daddy and Mother as he came into the breakfast nook.

"Thank you," smiled Glenn. Then he stared in surprise at the big, blue wagon standing by the table. "Oh, goody, goody!" he shouted, jumping up and down. "Thanks! It's just what I wanted! It's even bigger than Fred's or Jack's. Won't we three have fun with our wagons. I'll call it my fun wagon."

Daddy laughed. "You're quite welcome, son. I hope you will have lots of fun with your wagon. If you keep your eyes open, you can make it a helpful wagon, too, as well as a fun wagon."

After breakfast, Daddy went to the office,

and Glenn hurried out to feed his rabbits and bantams. Then he went riding with his wagon on the sidewalks and around the lawn. After a while, he decided a long ride would be more fun.

He ran into the kitchen. "Mother, may I take my fun wagon over to show Jack and Fred?"

Mother looked thoughtful. "I need some nice flat rocks and some rich soil for the rock garden. I thought perhaps we could walk out to Mr. Baker's farm and get some. Would you like that?"

Glenn frowned. "But, Mother, that would make my wagon dirty."

"We could lay paper in it and put the soil in buckets," she suggested.

"Aw, Mother, that wouldn't be any fun. Please let me go and have some fun with my fun wagon."

Mother smiled wistfully. "Very well, it would be nice for you to have fun on your birthday. I wanted to work in the rock garden today. But maybe I can get Mr. Baker's son to bring the rocks over. So run along and have a nice time."

Glenn dashed out the gate and started down the street. His mother's disappointment made him a little uncomfortable. Then he remembered what Daddy had said, and a little voice seemed to ask, "Is your wagon going to be a fun wagon or a helpful wagon?" But he was so eager to see what Jack and Fred would say about his wagon, that he hurried right on.

When he came to the foot of Hill Street, he met Mrs. Fike. She was carrying a big bag of groceries in one arm and leading Johnny with the other. Johnny was crying and saying, "I's tired, Mommy. Tarry me."

"I can't, dear. The groceries are too heavy," Mrs. Fike explained. Johnny sat right down in the middle of the sidewalk and wailed.

Glenn stopped and looked at him. "Hello, Johnny," he said. But Johnny wouldn't even look up. So Glenn went on.

After he had gone a little way, he turned and looked back. Mrs. Fike had coaxed Johnny to his feet and was half dragging him along. "I's tired, Mommy," Johnny was crying. He did look tired. His face was flushed, and his curls clung damply to his forehead.

"Why not help her?" a little voice seemed to whisper. It took Glenn only a minute to decide what to do. He turned around and hurried back to Mrs. Fike.

"How would you like to ride in my new wagon, Johnny?" he asked.

Johnny smiled through his tears and his blue eyes sparkled. "Ride, ride! Johnny ride," he shouted.

Mrs. Fike's worried expression broke into a happy smile. "How kind of you," she exclaimed. She set Johnny in the wagon. There was room to spare.

"Put the groceries in, too, and I'll pull them home for you," Glenn offered.

Even though the new, blue wheels turned easily, the groceries and the chubby little boy were quite a load to pull up Hill Street. Glenn's cheeks grew red, and his dark hair became moist with perspiration. But he kept right on going till he reached Mrs. Fike's door.

"Thank you so much," she said. "I didn't know how I was ever going to get up that hill with the groceries and Johnny. But with your kind help it was easy."

Glenn smiled at Mrs. Fike. "You're very welcome," he said.

Glenn had a happy feeling as he hurried home. On his way he thought of several other things he could do with his helpful wagon. It would be fun to haul things from the garden for Mother.

When he got home he found his mother behind the house. "Did you call Mr. Baker yet?" he asked.

Mother looked surprised. "No, I haven't. But I thought you went to play with Jack and Fred. Aren't they at home?"

Glenn grinned. "I don't know, Mother," he answered. "But I decided to make my birthday wagon a helpful wagon. I came back to help you get the soil and rocks, and then the tomatoes from the garden. I can play later."

Mother smiled. This time it was a happy smile.

BUNNY CHASE

Bobby changed into his after-school clothes and listened to the loud ticking of the clock. "It's too quiet in here," he said to himself. "I'll go outside and play with the rabbits till Mother comes home from the sewing circle."

When he stooped to look into the rabbits' pen, his blue eyes opened wide. Not one rabbit was there! Jumping to his feet, he ran behind the pen to look in the tall grass. They were not there either. Then he saw the grass shaking behind the garage. He ran over to see what was making it move.

There Bobby found Mrs. Snow and her four babies nibbling grass. When they saw him coming, they hopped under the fence into farmer Miller's clover field.

Oh my! thought Bobby, *how will I ever catch them? I wish Daddy or Mother were here.* He tried to squeeze under the fence, but his shirt caught on the barbed wire. *Rrrriiip.* A big hole tore into the back of his shirt.

At last he wiggled loose and got through the fence. "Come, bunnies," he coaxed. The rabbits only hopped farther away. Bobby began to run after them. His shirttail came out and flapped in the wind. His face grew red, and beads of perspiration came out on his freckled nose. By flopping flat on his tummy, he finally managed to grab the mother rabbit's leg.

Panting for breath, he picked himself up and held onto Mrs. Snow. "Come Frisky, Flippy, Floppy, and Mopsy," he coaxed. "Here's your mother."

The little rabbits stretched their furry, white necks, wiggled their noses, and blinked their pink eyes as if to say, "Where are you taking her?" Then they went right on nibbling clover.

Bobby knew he could not squeeze under the fence with a big rabbit in his arms. Holding onto Mrs. Snow with one hand, he put his other hand on top of the fence post and began to climb up. It was hard to keep his balance and swing his leg across the barbed wire. The seat of his jeans caught. *Rrrriiip!* Bobby frowned.

"Another hole in my clothes," he mumbled. He reached down to loosen his jeans. Suddenly Mrs. Snow took a big leap. Away she hopped—back to the clover field.

Bobby jumped down and stood staring after her. He was hot and tired. He felt like crying. With both hands he dabbed at the tears that wanted to spill from his eyes. He had been so busy holding onto the rabbit that he hadn't noticed a shiny blue car stopping beside the road.

"Hello, Bobby. Do you need help?" asked a kind voice.

Bobby jumped. Dabbing once more at the tears, he looked up into the friendly brown eyes of Pastor Maust. Quickly he tried to cover the hole in his jeans with one hand. *What will the pastor think?* he wondered. *I can't ask him to help me. His job is preaching and visiting sick folks, not catching rabbits.*

"I . . . I . . . guess not," he stammered. "My rabbits got out, and I'm afraid a dog might get them before Mother comes home."

"I guessed that's what happened when I saw you trying to climb the fence with a big white rabbit," smiled Pastor Maust. "Come, I'll help you get them."

Bobby glanced doubtfully at Pastor Maust's good suit. "You might get dirty or tear your clothes," he protested.

"Never mind," Pastor Maust laughed. "I'll be careful. Now let's see. Do you have a box we could put the rabbits into when we catch them?"

"Sure," said Bobby. "Why didn't I think of that?" He ran to the garage for a box.

Pastor Maust held the fence down and stepped across in one big swing. Then he held the wires apart so that Bobby could climb through without getting scratched.

When the rabbits saw Bobby and the pastor coming, they hop-hop-hopped farther away. Pastor Maust set the box down and ran ahead to chase them back.

"Stand just beyond the box and maybe they will go into it," he directed Bobby. Bobby stood right at the place Pastor Maust pointed to.

Bobby watched as Pastor Maust gently shooed the rabbits toward the box. It seemed strange to see him out in the field. Of course he always shook Bobby's hand and said hello after church. But somehow, Bobby had never noticed before how friendly he was. He thought he was acting very much like Daddy would if Daddy were there. In fact, he thought that next to Daddy, Pastor Maust was the nicest man he knew. He couldn't help smiling when Pastor Maust made a grab for Mopsy and missed her.

Suddenly Mrs. Snow came hopping right up to the box and jumped in. Frisky, Flippy, Floppy, and Mopsy followed her. Bobby flipped the lid shut. Forgetting to be shy, he jumped up and down shouting, "There they are, all five of them!"

Pastor Maust laughed. "Sure enough," he agreed, walking to the fence. He picked up the box, swung it across, and set it on the ground. After he held the wires apart for Bobby to get through, he swung across himself. Pastor Maust picked up the box, and they walked to the pen together.

Paster Maust examined the pen and found a hole in the netting. "We'll have to mend this or your rabbits won't stay at home," he said.

"There's some leftover netting in the garage. I'll get it and a hammer and staples," offered Bobby. In a minute he was back.

Pastor Maust showed Bobby how to make a strong splice. He stapled the netting fast at the bottom of the pen. Then he lifted the box, and Bobby chased the rabbits into their pen.

Bobby felt like hugging Pastor Maust. "Oh, thank you. I'm so glad you came."

Pastor Maust rumpled Bobby's brown hair. "So am I, Bobby. It was fun to catch the rabbits."

Then he brushed some white fur from his coat and smoothed back his thick black hair. Suddenly he tapped Bobby's shoulder. "You're it!" he said, and raced away to his car. And with a friendly wave, he drove away.

Bobby had been too surprised to run after him. While he stood staring after the car, Mother drove in. He skipped over to tell her what had happened. "Pastor Maust really is a nice man," he added. "And he tagged me *it* as he left. But just wait, I'll get him back the first chance I have."

THE FOUR TINY T'S

James dashed out of the shop door and raced toward the drive. "Stop! Daddy, stop," he yelled. "Come quick. Polly's gone and her babies are dead!"

Daddy stopped the car and got out. "Are you sure?" He hurried to the shop. "Probably Polly just decided to look for a new home and is hidden somewhere in the shop."

James was right. Polly was gone. A freshly gnawed hole in the back of the cage was the only clue to what had happened to her. They looked behind the door, under the workbench, through piles of lumber, in nail kegs—everywhere a hamster could hide. But they could not find a trace of Polly.

Just then Thomas, their neighbor's big black cat, came slinking into the shop. He sat inside the shop door and began to wash himself.

James shook his fist at him. "Did you eat my

pet hamster?" he yelled. Thomas flattened his ears and blinked his eyes. When James noticed the cat's bulging sides, he stamped his foot and shouted, "Scat!" With a wild leap, Thomas sailed outside.

"Easy," soothed Daddy. "We can't prove that Thomas ate Polly." Daddy turned back to Polly's cage. "Let's take a look at Polly's babies."

He lifted the lid of the nest box to touch one of the scrawny hamsters. It wiggled and began squeaking in a weak, hungry voice. Then the rest began to squeak and squirm.

"They're hungry. We will have to see what we can do for them." Daddy picked up the box and carried it to the house where Mother was feeding Tammy, James's baby sister. James told Mother the whole story.

"We can try feeding them the baby's formula in a bottle," Mother suggested.

Dianna ran to get Betsy-Doll's bottle. James washed it and filled it with formula. Then he poked the nipple into a tiny, pink hamster mouth. At first the hamster chewed and tried to spit the nipple out. But when he tasted warm milk, he began sucking with all his might. His hollow sides grew round. He dropped the nipple, curled up, and went to sleep. One by one, three more babies drank greedily, curled up, and went to sleep.

At bedtime the hamsters were crying again. James fed them and put their box right by his bed so that he would hear them if they got hungry during the night. At two o'clock when Tammy awoke for her bottle, the hamsters were crying too. James sat up on the edge of the bed and rubbed his eyes. He shook himself awake and stumbled out to the kitchen. He warmed the bottle, dived under the covers, and leaned out across the bed to feed his hungry babies.

Every day at noon, James dashed home from school to feed the hamsters. How they loved milk! James bought more doll bottles at the store. He asked Daddy to help bore slanting holes into the hamsters' box just large enough to slip the bottle tops through. Now when his family got hungry, he just popped a bottle of milk into each hole. The hamsters grew fast, and soon James could tell them apart by their coats of brown fur.

"I'll name them Teeny, Tiny, Tony, and Tommy and call them the T's for short," he decided. By this time the T's were nibbling some cabbage and pellets. But every night when Tammy awoke for her bottle, they called for theirs too.

One night Tammy forgot to wake up. The T's slept on too! After that, neither Mother nor James had to feed their babies at night.

As the T's grew, they became more and more curious and bold. One day when James came home from school, they had all climbed out of their box. He soon found Teeny, Tiny, and Tony asleep under his bed. He searched and called and called and searched for Tommy, but Tommy could not be found.

After supper the whole family, except Tammy, got down on their knees to look in closets, behind radiators, under beds, everywhere. It was no use. Tommy did not appear. "He was the cutest of them all," sighed James.

"Never mind," Mother said. "He can't get out of the house. Let's ask God to help us find him."

James kicked off his shoes and poked his toes into his left bedroom slipper.

Suddenly he screamed, "Eeeks!" and kicked the slipper across the room. A brown ball flew out of the slipper and uncurled. Daddy, Mother, and Dianna came running to see what had happened. How they laughed! James picked Tommy up gently.

"I'm sorry, little fellow," James apologized. "God sure helped us find him in a hurry," he said, laughing.

Daddy looked at Mother, and Mother looked at Daddy. "I think it's time the T's move out to Polly's cage," they said together.

So the next day Daddy patched the hole, and Teeny, Tiny, Tony, and Tommy moved to Polly's old cage. They loved to scamper and explore all around their new home. James brought them fresh greens, water, and pellets every day.

About a month later, Teeny and Tiny did not come to meet James when he brought them their breakfast. He opened the nest box and looked in. Quickly dropping the lid, he ran toward the house, calling. "Daddy, Mother, Dianna, come here!"

Mother turned off the burners on the stove. Daddy laid down the morning paper. Everyone followed James to the shop. He stood back and laughed at their surprised faces when they saw Teeny and Tiny in the nest box, each nursing three babies.

"Well," said James, "it was fun playing mother for Teeny and Tiny, but they can have that job this time."

THE MISSED BOAT RIDE

It was Saturday morning, and Elsie knew that her small cleaning tasks were to be done before she started reading her new book. She walked over to the bookshelf and picked up *Snuggles.* How smooth the cover was, and the white kitten in a dress was really cute.

Just then Mother called from the kitchen,"Elsie, please do the dusting in the living room before Cindy wakes up. I'll need you to watch her while I finish these pies for the fellowship dinner tomorrow."

Elsie opened the book to page one. "Coming, Mother," she called. The color photo of a row of kittens all dressed up was so interesting that she just couldn't lay the book down. She took the dust cloth from the cleaning closet, flipped another page, and walked slowly to the living room, reading as she went.

Noticing how thin the book was, she thought, I*t won't take long to read this. I'll do* *the dusting real fast afterwards.* She sat on the edge of the sofa and tried to read rapidly.

Big words like Snuggle's real name, Gwendolyn Daphne Stella Arabella Marguerite, slowed her reading. By the time Elsie had read about Snuggle's parents, Tilly and Willy, her little sister Squeak, and her friends, Tim, Tam, Tom, and Tabby, Elsie's own little sister, Cindy, began to cry.

"Are you finished with the dusting?" called Mother. "I'm right in the middle of filling pumpkin pies."

"Jus . . . just about," answered Elsie. "I'll get Cindy."

I'll hurry so fast that mother won't even know I haven't started, she assured herself.

Elsie went to the nursery, lowered the side of the crib, and with a mighty heave, lifted Cindy down to the floor. She was cross and toddled to the kitchen where she clung to Mother's skirt, crying to be picked up.

Elsie tossed her pigtails back. "Come, Cindy, do you want to ride in the wagon?" she coaxed. Cindy stopped crying and took hold of Elsie's slender finger with her chubby hand.

Outside, Elsie put her into the little red wagon. "Hold tight," she instructed. Cindy's cheeks grew pink, and her blue eyes sparkled. Their pink dresses flapped in the warm summer breeze.

They played happily until lunchtime. After lunch Elsie helped Mother with the dishes. Just as she was ready to hurry to the living room and do the dusting, she heard her little friends, Lisa and Linda, calling outside. "Elsie, Mother is taking us for a walk in the meadow. Do you want to come along?" they asked.

Elsie skipped to the door, her brown eyes sparkling. "Sure thing! I'll ask Mother," she said. Turning she said, "May I, Mother?"

Mother brushed back a stray lock of hair. "Did you finish the dusting in the living room?" she asked.

Elsie stooped to tie her blue sneaker. "Uh, umm hum," she stammered, "it's all finished."

"All right, you may go," smiled Mother. "Have a nice time."

Mrs. Baker, Elsie, and the twins followed a winding path along the creek. They found wild roses, columbine, and primroses blooming on the bank. When they grew tired, they sat on a log under a shady maple tree. A pair of robins scolded them.

Lisa laughed. "It sounds as if they were saying fibs, fibs," she said. "Who fibs, Mr. Robin?" she asked. "Not us; the Bible tells us not to tell lies."

Immediately Elsie thought of the neglected dusting. *I hope Mother doesn't find out. I'll do it first thing when I get home,* she promised herself.

The robins continued to scold. Elsie's cheeks grew hot. *It does sound like fibs. I wish they'd be quiet,* she thought. She was glad Mrs. Baker suggested moving on so as not to worry the birds.

On the way home, they saw a killdeer, dragging its wing as though it were hurt. "Oh look, she's crippled," cried Lisa.

"She's not really hurt," Mrs. Baker explained. "She's trying to lead us away from her babies that are probably close by."

"Don't worry, Mrs. Killdeer," she continued. "We won't harm your little ones."

When Elsie was nearly back home, she was surprised to see her cousins Billy and Joy from Ohio come running to meet her. "Hi, Elsie," they called. "We're going boating up at Little Meadows Lake. We stopped to see if you could go along."

Elsie's brown eyes sparkled. "Ohooo! I love boating. Come on, let's ask my mother." On the way to the house she remembered the neglected dusting and hoped Mother hadn't discovered it.

The three children came to the house just in time to hear Mother tell Aunt Jessie and Uncle Fred, "I'm so glad you stopped in. And it's very nice of you to offer to take Elsie along, but she has some duties here at home she needs to take care of."

Elsie's face burned, and her eyes smarted. One glance at Mother told Elsie that Mother had discovered the dusty living room.

"We could wait for Elsie," offered Joy

"Sorry, but she can't go this time," Mother said with a note of finality.

In a few minutes, Uncle Freds were pulling

out of the drive with Joy and Billy waving and calling from the open windows, "We wish you could come along, Elsie."

As soon as they were gone, Mother led Elsie to the living room. "I'm very sorry you were untruthful about the dusting, Elsie. It would have been all right to leave it until you came home if you had told me the truth. But since you deceived me, you will need to do it now as well as miss your boat ride."

Elsie's eyes blinked. Suddenly she burst into tears. "I'm sorry, Mother. Please forgive me," she sobbed.

Mother drew her close. "I surely will, dear. Shall we ask God to forgive you and help you to be truthful?"

"Yes," nodded Elsie. Together they bowed their heads and prayed for forgiveness. Elsie looked up with a smile and gave Mother a hug. "I'll do the dusting right away," she said.

DOUBLE-DUTY DALE

Mrs. Martin glanced at the second graders preparing for dismissal and cleared her throat. "Roger Smith broke his kneecap when he fell on the playground Friday," she said. "He won't be able to come to school for at least a month. Will someone volunteer to take his assignments to him every evening and help him with his lessons?"

Jimmy looked at Dale, Dale looked at Charles, and Charles looked at Jimmy. "How about one of you boys that live out his way on Elm Avenue?" asked Mrs. Martin.

Charles squirmed in his seat and slowly shook his head.

"Not me," said Jimmy with a vigorous shake of his head.

Dale scratched behind his ear and rumpled his brown hair. "I . . . I guess I can," he offered.

"Fine," said Mrs. Martin, smiling. "Roger's mother picked up his books today, and I gave her his assignments, but I didn't have time to explain the new problems. So your duties begin this evening."

On the way home, Jimmy said, "You won't catch me doing double duty like that. I get enough of school during the day. Just think of the fun you'll miss."

"Yeah," put in Charles, "who wants to stay in the house all evening?"

Dale blinked. "Of course I'd rather play too. But if I had a broken leg, I'd be mighty glad if someone came to help me with my lessons."

At home Dale explained the plan to his mother. She smiled approvingly. "That's fine, Dale. I'm glad you volunteered. Mrs. Smith has her hands full since her husband died. Taking care of four children and doing laundry for other people keeps her very busy. Now she won't have Roger to run errands and help her either."

In a few minutes Dale was ringing the doorbell at Roger's house. Freddy, Roger's brother, opened the door. "Hi, Dale. Come in. Mommy's washing and Roger's bawling 'cause he can't get his problems."

Freddy led Dale to the back room. Roger lay in faded pajamas, propped up with pillows on a bed. Only his toes stuck out of the thick white cast on his leg. Surrounding him were books and papers. Quickly he dabbed at the corners of his blue eyes and jammed a handkerchief under his pillows.

"Hi, Roger," Dale said cheerfully.

"Hi, Dale. I'm glad you came. I just can't get these problems, and Mother's so rushed to get Mrs. Jones' laundry ready, she can't help me."

Soon Dale's and Roger's heads were bent over the problems. "Here's the trouble," Dale pointed out. "You have to borrow." Carefully he explained the steps of borrowing.

"Oh, I see," Roger cried. "That will be fun now that I understand it. I can do it tomorrow."

"All right. Let's take turns pronouncing our spelling words to each other," suggested Dale. The boys were surprised to find how soon they knew how to spell their words.

Then Roger's mother came into the room. "I don't like to leave you alone with the children, but there's no other way. Will you boys watch and entertain them while I deliver Mrs. Jones' laundry?"

Dale jumped up. "Let me deliver it. I know where she lives, and I'd love to take it."

"Oh, would you?" beamed Mrs. Smith. "That would be wonderful!"

After shrugging into his blue jacket, Dale started off down the street with the basket of laundry on Roger's red wagon.

Charles and Jimmy met him on their roller

skates. "Here comes double-duty Dale," jeered Jimmy, "carting a load of laundry instead of having fun."

Dale didn't say anything. He lugged the basket up on the porch and rang the doorbell. Crippled Mrs. Jones came to open the door in her wheelchair. "Well, how nice of you to help out Mrs. Smith, now that Roger is laid up," she smiled. "Just set the basket up on this little bench, and I'll be able to reach it."

Dale felt warm inside as he hurried back to Roger's house.

"Thank you so much," said Mrs. Smith earnestly.

"You're welcome. It was fun," Dale answered. "Let me do the delivering for you until Roger can do it again. I can do it when I bring his assignments over."

"I'll appreciate it so much if you can." Mrs. Smith smiled gratefully.

Dale went back to help Roger with the new reading words. Suddenly he noticed that it was getting dark. "I'll have to go home for supper," he exclaimed. "I'll be back tomorrow night."

For the next few weeks, Dale was very busy. He had so much fun romping with Roger's baby sister and brothers that he didn't mind not getting to play with Charles and Jimmy. They continued to tease him every evening as he delivered laundry to different people. "Double-duty Dale, Double-duty Dale," they called out to him. Dale didn't like it.

On the fourth Friday, Mrs. Martin and Miss Bender, the third grade teacher, planned a hike and picnic right after school. Dale heard the boys discussing the fun they would have.

"I'll beat you to the picnic grounds, Dale," Jimmy boasted.

"I can't go," Dale said wistfully. "Roger's mother is depending on me to deliver Mrs. Jones' laundry after school."

"Huh!" snorted Jimmy and Charles. "Forget your duties tonight. You can do that tomorrow. This is a school activity. You should go along."

Maybe they're right, Dale thought on his way home. As he got off the bus and watched it disappear with the rest of the class for their hike and picnic in the country, he blinked back tears. Dragging his feet, he came into the kitchen. "I wish I could have gone along," he told Mother.

"It's too bad they couldn't postpone it until Roger could go," Mother agreed. "But this nice fall weather will not last long."

Taking Roger's assignments, Dale went over to the Smiths. Roger's mother met him at the door. "Would you mind delivering Mrs. Jones' laundry first thing?" she asked.

"No, ma'am," Dale answered cheerfully. He trudged off, whistling, with the baskets of laundry.

When he returned, he was surprised to see Mr. Martin sitting in his car in the Smith driveway. Inside the house, his teacher, Mrs. Martin, was talking to Roger's mother. Mrs.

Martin flashed a smile at Dale. "Not only has Roger kept up with his class," she was telling Roger's mother, "but Dale and he have both worked their grades up so that they are at the head of the class."

Turning to the boys she said, "How would you boys like to join us on the hike and picnic?"

Roger and Dale looked at each other, astonished. Mrs. Martin laughed. "Yes, it's all right. I checked with your doctor, Roger. Mr. Martin will take you out to the car."

"Yippee, goody, goody!" shouted Dale and Roger.

Mr. Martin carried Roger out to the car and away they went. Catching up with the hikers, he stopped the car. "Do you want to walk with the other children, Dale?" he asked.

Dale looked at Roger. "Sure, go ahead," said Roger, nodding. "I'll be looking for you at the picnic grounds."

Dale bounced out and raced ahead to join the other children. "Doing double duty wasn't too bad," he told himself.

COLOR QUARRELS

Donna's usually sunny face was sober as she watched the rain streaking down the playroom window. Tossing back her red pigtails, she took her paper dolls off the shelf. "Let's play school with the paper dolls Aunt Ruth gave us for our birthdays," she suggested.

"Good," agreed Doris, tossing back her red pigtails and reaching for her dolls. "We can put them all together and pretend we have a whole family of twins."

Donna's brown eyes sparkled. "That will be fun if we can think of enough twin names," she laughed.

Out came the identical sets of dolls and their paper clothes. There were big sisters Hilda and Hazel, middle-sized brothers Tom and Tony, little sisters Sharon and Shirley, and kindergarten-sized Peter and Perry, to be named and dressed.

"It's morning. Time for lazy Tom and Tony

to get up, or they will be late to school," giggled Donna. "Then when our doll family comes home from school, we'll have a birthday party for Sharon and Shirley," she planned.

What fun they had getting their doll family ready for school. Each girl did the talking for her own dolls.

Mother, who was crocheting in the easy chair, chuckled when Tony raced down the street so fast that his clothes flew off, and he had to come back and get dressed again.

After a while Mother laid her crocheting aside. "I had better get supper started," she said, starting out to the kitchen.

After the dolls were through all their classes in school, Donna and Doris took them home. "Now we'll have the party for Sharon and Shirley," said Doris. "Let's put Hilda and Hazel's green dresses on them for the party."

"Green dresses?" exclaimed Donna. "They don't have any green dresses."

"Sure they do, see here," said Doris, holding up the dress she wanted Hazel to wear to the party.

"Huh! That's not green. It's blue," declared Donna.

"It's not blue, it's green!" insisted Doris.

"No, it isn't," Donna almost shouted. "It's no more green than you are, so there!"

The corners of Doris's mouth turned down and her dimples vanished. "Smarty, smarty! You always think you know best," she retorted.

"Smarty, smarty, yourself," Donna snapped

back, her face red and her dimples hidden behind a big frown. Angry words bounced back and forth like hailstones on a tin roof.

Mother quickly popped the potatoes into the oven and hurried back to the playroom. For a moment she just stood there looking at the two scowling faces and listening to their unkind words. The girls were so busy shouting and frowning, that they didn't even notice her standing there.

Grabbing up all her dolls, Donna shouted, "All right, if you're so smart, you can have your old dolls and have your own party just for them!"

"Girls, girls, what is the trouble?" asked Mother. "When I left this room five minutes ago, you were playing happily. Now it seems you have moved to Fussing Avenue in Quarrelville!"

"Donna insists that this dress is blue," snapped Doris, holding out the offending dress. "Say it's green, Mother!"

"Say it's blue, Mother," interrupted Donna.

Mother shook her head. "Well, well, is that what my girls are quarreling about? You are both wrong. That color is a mixture of green and blue called aqua. Did you forget that the Bible says we should forgive each other instead of quarreling?"

Donna's brown eyes looked at the floor. Doris's brown eyes looked at the floor. Big frowns still hid their dimples.

"You two were saying very unkind things to

each other. Don't you think you should apologize?" Mother suggested.

Donna's brown eyes looked into Doris's brown eyes, and Doris's brown eyes looked into Donna's. The corners of their mouths began to twitch. "I'm sorry I said nasty things to you, Doris," said Donna, a smile spreading over her face.

"I'm sorry for the things I said too," added Doris, a smile putting her dimples back into place.

"That's better, girls," said Mother with a warm smile. "You know, girls, your quarrel reminds me of a song your great-grandmother used to sing to Grandma and her sisters when they quarreled. It's called the song of Dan and Dimple. Listen to it.

To begin with things quite simple,
Quarrels never fail:
Once they fell out—Dan and Dimple,
All about a horse's tail.
So that by and by this quarrel
Quite broke up and spoilt their play.
Dan said the tail was sorrel,
Dimple said that it was gray.

Chorus

Dan said the tail was sorrel.
Dimple said that it was gray.
So that by and by this quarrel
Quite broke up and spoilt their play.

In between them came their mother,
What is all this fuss about?
Then the sister and the brother
Told the story out and out.
Then she answered I must label
Each of you a little dunce,
Since a look within the stable
Would have settled it at once.

Forth ran Dan and Dimple after,
And they soon came hurrying back,
Shouting, all aglee with laughter,
That the horse's tail was BLACK.
So they both agreed to profit
By the lesson they had learned
And to tell each other of it
Often as such fits returned.

Doris looked at Donna with a sheepish grin. Donna looked at Doris with a sheepish grin. "It does sound like us," they admitted. "The next time we feel a quarrel coming, we'll remember Dan and Dimple."

COALS OF FIRE

Billy Lee reached up and gave Marie's long red pigtails a hard jerk. Marie ignored him and went right ahead with her arithmetic assignment. As she jotted down the last number, Billy gave her arm a hard shove, leaving a heavy black line right through the center of her paper.

"Billy!" hissed Marie. "You mean boy! Look what you did!"

Miss Calhoun whirled around from the blackboard where she was helping Johnny with a problem. "Who whispered?" she demanded sternly.

Marie's chubby face turned red but she didn't say a word. "Who whispered?" repeated Miss Calhoun.

Billy pointed to Marie sitting right in front of him.

Her cheeks grew even redder. A frown crossed Miss Calhoun's face. "Did you whisper, Marie?" she asked. Marie nodded slowly.

"Bring your reader up here to study until recess," commanded Miss Calhoun.

Angry tears smarted in Marie's brown eyes as she stumbled to the front of the room. Holding her book in front of her face, she tried to study. *I wish Billy Lee would move back to the city where he came from,* she thought.

After school Peggy and Alice walked home with Marie. "I think that Billy Lee is the meanest boy in school," Peggy declared.

"Is that so?" sneered Billy, darting out from behind a tree. "Ho, ho, ho! Teacher's pet had to sit up front today." With a quick move, he tripped Marie.

Her books flew in all directions. Bursting into sobs, she scrambled to pick herself up. "Cry baby, cry baby," chanted Billy. Then seeing Dick, Marie's third-grade brother, and his chums coming, Billy dashed down the street.

While Marie brushed the dust off her dress and wiped blood from her knees, Alice and Peggy gathered up her books.

"What happened?" Dick asked.

"Billy Lee tripped me," sobbed Marie.

Dick's usually soft brown eyes snapped. "I'll get him one of these days if he doesn't stop pestering you," he threatened. "Here, let me carry your books." Dick and Marie walked home together. In the kitchen they poured out the whole story to Mother, who was baking cookies. Mother stopped to clean up Marie's bleeding knees and listen sympathetically to the sad tale.

Dick thrust his hands deep into his pockets and shoved out his chest. "I'd like to knock some sense into Billy's head!" he declared.

Mother sighed and shook her head. The children were startled to see her eyes fill with tears. "I don't think that's what he needs. Billy's mother was my best friend. She died when he was born. Poor Billy has never had a happy home. He's been shifted from relative to relative and school to school until he's a grade behind. He's just two days younger than Dick."

"How awful," gasped Marie. "But what can we do? He's so mean!"

"Right now he's staying with his crippled, nearly blind grandmother. She does the best she can, but Billy needs love and attention," said Mother. "Coals of fire may be the best way to reach him."

Dick and Marie stared at Mother. "What do you mean?"

"The Bible teaches us that returning kindness for evil is like heaping coals of fire on a person's head," Mother explained.

"Oh, yes, we remember," the children said, nodding.

"Is there anything that Billy likes especially well or does well?" Mother wondered.

Marie rubbed her forehead hard the way she always did when she was thinking. "He doesn't play much. The children don't choose him for games. Oh, I know. He's always looking at bird books, and he wins every time we have a bird quiz. Could we take him along on our bird hike, Mother?"

"That's a fine idea," said Mother, smiling as she slid a pan of animal-shaped cookies out of the oven.

Suddenly Marie's face lit up. "Say, could we make a cardinal-shaped cookie and frost it with red frosting?" she asked.

"We can at least try," Mother agreed.

"I'll try to get Billy to play with us third graders," added Dick. "Maybe he'll get along better with us boys."

The next morning Marie carried a bag with the cellophane-wrapped cardinal and two oranges in it.

"Teacher's pet, teacher's pet," chanted Billy, catching up with her. "You got something in your bag for teacher, huh?"

Marie's cheeks grew hot. She wanted to run ahead and keep the bag. But remembering the "coals of fire" plan, she thought, *Please, Jesus, help me to be kind and pleasant.*

Then smiling, she held out the bag. "No, Billy, it's a surprise for you."

Billy stopped short. Blinking his cold, blue eyes he finally stammered, "D . . . d . . . do you mean it?"

"Of course!" Marie thrust the bag into his grimy hands.

Clutching it as though he were afraid it might vanish, Billy peeked in. "Hey, a cardinal cookie—and oranges," he squealed. "I'll share this with Granny."

Just then Dick caught up with them. "Say, Billy, Marie says you know a lot about birds. Want to go on a bird hike with our family and help us identify the birds we see?"

Billy's eyes sparkled and a wide smile spread over his face. "I sure will if Granny can spare me," he said. "I'll let you know tomorrow."

All day Billy grinned shyly every time he met Marie.

Next morning Billy came racing to meet Dick and Marie. "I can go," he shouted.

"Good," said Dick. "We'll pick you up at 5:30."

Marie smiled as the boys ran ahead like old friends. "I do believe the 'coals of fire' are really working," she told herself.

CHRISTMAS BUNDLE FUN

Snip, snip, snip, went Mother's scissors. "Oh, what are you doing with that cloth with the pink roses?" asked Peggy.

"I want to make Christmas bundle dresses to send overseas. The sweaters Daddy got go in bundles for five- and seven-year-old girls. So there will be one just your size and one Ruth's size," answered Mother.

Peggy's face clouded as though a storm were coming, "Please make a dress like that for me too," she begged.

"Me too," said Ruth, coming to see.

"Well," explained Mother, "I believe you have all the dresses you need. Don't you think it would be nice to give these to some little girls who need them? Some little girls have only one dress, and they have to go to bed while their mother washes it."

"Yes," agreed sunny little Ruth, showing her dimples. She ran back to play with her doll.

Peggy still looked very sober. "Why didn't you get enough of that material to make dresses for us too?" she grumbled.

Snip, snip, snip went the scissors. Still Peggy pouted.

"There, that is finished," said Mother. "And there is enough material left to make a dress for each of the dolls Daddy brought home."

Peggy's red pigtails bounced as she jumped off her chair and ran to get the dolls for Mother. Her pouting stopped when she thought of the dolls.

Mother cut out the doll dresses and soon the sewing machine was humming. First the big dresses were finished. The girls tried them on while Mother sewed the doll's dresses.

"Could I sew the buttons on?" asked Peggy.

"I believe you could if I help you," decided Mother.

"Let me sew buttons too," said Ruth.

Mother threaded three needles, and everyone began to sew. Suddenly Ruth pricked her finger. Her eyes got big and round. "I'm done sewing now," she said, as she handed her work to Mother. Peggy kept right on sewing until the last button was fast.

"Thank you. You were good help," smiled Mother. Peggy's brown eyes beamed with delight.

"Now I will take some of this pink flannel

and make bunting blankets for the dolls," said Mother. How cute the dolls looked when they were all dressed up.

"Won't those little girls be surprised when they find their dolls have dresses just like their own?" exclaimed Peggy.

By the time tall Jason and chubby Jacob came home from school, everything was finished, and they began to pack the bundles.

"We will get the clothes you made for the boys' bundles," offered Jason. Soon they had everything together: towels, soap, clothing, handkerchiefs, balls for the boys' bundles, and dolls for the girls, and a pretty Christmas greeting for each one.

The children helped Mother place everything on the towels and watched as she wrapped and pinned them securely with safety pins, ready to be shipped overseas. The dolls still cried when the bundles were squeezed.

"Girls can easily guess what is in their bundles," exclaimed Peggy. "But the balls won't talk when they are squeezed. This was more fun than getting a new dress for myself," she added happily.

AN IMPORTANT NOSE

Betty dried the last plate, put it into the cupboard, and glanced out the window. She watched the girl across the street jumping rope.

"Mother," she said, "may I invite Carol over to help me put my birthday puzzle together? Jean and Peggy say they are glad she didn't move next door to them. They are afraid she'd take something because her daddy was in jail for stealing. But I think Carol is a nice girl."

Mother looked up from the spicy cake batter she was mixing. "Surely you may, Betty. I'm glad you feel that way about her. After all, Carol can't help what her father did."

Betty skipped to the telephone. Ten minutes later the girls were sitting at the little red table, putting the puzzle together. Slowly but surely the picture grew. At last they could see the outline of a baby peeping out of a blue blanket.

"What's this funny-looking piece?" Betty asked, handing a piece to Carol.

Carol turned it this way and that way and over again.

"I know," she cried. "It's the baby's nose. See, it's plain when you hold it this way. I'll lay it right here on the corner of the table so that we can find it when we're ready for it."

The pieces of the puzzle were hard to find because the colors were so much the same. The girls worked a long time to find the baby's bottle and a brown puppy chewing a shoe. Carol tossed back her blond hair and leaned back in her chair to rest. Betty got up and stretched her tired back. Finally they had the baby's face nearly completed.

"Now where's that nosepiece?" asked Betty.

Carol looked at the edge of the table. She got up and shook her yellow dress. They looked under the table and on the chairs. But they couldn't find that important nosepiece.

Remembering what Jean and Peggy had said, Betty looked at Carol and wondered. But then she suggested, "Let's put all the rest together and maybe we'll find it."

Finally every piece except the nose was in place. Only a hole showed where the nose should have been. Again Betty looked at Carol suspiciously.

"It never will look right without that piece," she sighed. "What did you do with it?"

Carol's thin face flushed. "I laid it right here. You saw me."

"But it isn't there now. You put it somewhere else because I don't have it," Betty argued. "Where is it?"

Carol's blue eyes began to blink, and her chin quivered. "I don't know where it is," she burst out. "Just because my daddy was in jail, you think I took it. I'm going home. I don't want to play with you if you think I'm a thief."

Betty's mouth dropped open as she watched Carol dash out the door. She ran to the window to watch Carol burst into her own house across the street. But Betty couldn't hear Carol's sobs.

"Betty's just like the girls in Springdale were," Carol told her mother between tears. "She thinks I'm a thief. Why would I want one little old piece of her puzzle?" The whole story tumbled out.

Mrs. Yaste sighed. "It's hard to understand why people suspect us because of Daddy's mistake. Maybe Betty will find that important nosepiece and decide to be friends after all."

Carol wiped her eyes. "Even if she does find it, I won't be her friend. She blamed me for stealing."

"Remember, Carol," her mother said gently, "if we want others to forget what Daddy did, we will have to do our share of forgiving and forgetting too."

After Carol had left, Betty sat staring at the puzzle. "Peggy and Jean were right," she told herself. "Carol must have taken the piece. That's why she got so cross about it. Oh dear, the puzzle's ruined without a nose."

Betty curled up on the couch to read and forget about the puzzle. Suddenly she felt a big sneeze coming. She grabbed for her handkerchief. "Kerchoo!" As the handkerchief came out of her pocket, something else flew out of her pocket and landed on the floor. Betty walked over to see what it was.

For a moment she just stood and stared. Then she stooped and slowly picked up that important nose!

"I had that piece in my pocket and blamed Carol for taking it," she said aloud. "I must have brushed it off the table." She turned the piece over and over. At least she had all the pieces now!

Betty fitted the piece into place. Now the puzzle was finished. But something inside Betty reminded her how Carol must feel. Betty knew what she must do. She picked up the piece again and told her mother where she was going.

Just deciding to tell Carol made Betty feel better. By the time she reached the Yaste's porch, she was glad to ring the doorbell.

Carol opened the door. When she saw Betty, she frowned and began to close it again. Quickly Betty held up the piece of puzzle.

"Look, Carol. It was in my pocket. I'm awfully sorry I blamed you for taking it. May I play with you again?"

Betty watched Carol look from the puzzle piece to the floor and back again. Then slowly a smile crossed her face.

"Sure, Betty. Come in. We can play with my twin dolls."

A DANDY DAY FOR DONNA

Donna put the last plate into the cupboard and slammed the door so that the dishes rattled on the shelf. "It isn't fair," she grumbled. "I'm always either working or having to play with the children. I wish I were the only child in our family like Jane is in hers."

"You are the only Donna I have," Mother said. "I often thank God for you and that you are such a big help to me."

"But I can never do just what I want to. Jane can do just as she pleases most of the time."

A thoughtful smile crossed Mother's face. "Very well," she said. "Tomorrow will be your special day. You may pretend you are Jane and play alone all day."

"Oh, goody!" shouted Donna. "That will be dandy!" And she skipped right off to bed.

The next morning when Donna awoke, the sun was already high in the sky, and a robin was singing in a maple tree outside her window. Quickly she bounced out of bed. *I won't waste my dandy day sleeping,* she told herself.

The rest of the family had already eaten. Donna gulped her breakfast and then slipped right outside to play. What fun it was to do nothing in the kitchen.

The lawn seemed very quiet and empty. Donna got a book and curled up on the porch swing to read. After a while she got tired of reading.

Just then she heard the twins and Billy laughing behind the house. Slowly she walked back to see what they were doing. Mother was helping them build a farm in the sandpile.

"Oh, let me help," cried Donna.

"But you don't want to play with the children today," Mother reminded her. Donna turned and walked slowly back to the porch. She heard baby Jerry, who had just wakened from his nap, crying. Donna started in to get him. "Run along and play, dear. I'll take care of Jerry this time," Mother called.

Donna tried riding on the red wagon. But riding alone was no fun. After a while Mother came out and put Jerry into the playpen on the porch. She sat down on the swing to read the story of Jonah for Ruth, Rhoda, and Billy. Donna sat on the steps to listen. Jerry stretched his chubby arms toward her and cooed. How sweet he looked. Donna got up to take him.

Mother glanced up from her book. "Did you forget?" she asked. Donna sat down again. By and by Mother picked up Jerry and went into the house to get lunch.

"Let's play church, girls," Donna suggested.

"Oh, no," answered Ruth and Rhoda in one breath. "We are helping Mother today." Bouncing off the swing, they skipped into the house.

After lunch Donna didn't so much as glance at the dishes. "Come, Billy, and I'll give you a ride on the wagon," she offered.

Billy rolled his big blue eyes. "No," he said. "I don't want a ride."

Slowly walking back to the sandpile, Donna picked up a red truck and filled it with sand.

Suddenly Billy came racing out. "I want to play now. Go away," he shouted.

Donna was shocked. Then she remembered that Billy was only cooperating with her wish not to play with him. She walked back to the porch and plunked onto the swing. By and by she got up and peeped into the kitchen where the twins were drying dishes for Mother. Opening the door softly, she tiptoed right up to Mother.

"Mother," she whispered. "Please, may I help you and play with the children? I'm tired of being Jane."

In spite of her wet hands, Mother smiled and drew her close. "Certainly you may, dear."

Donna picked up a stack of clean dishes and

set them quietly on the shelf. Closing the door, she said, "Now I know why Jane likes to play with my little brothers and sisters when she comes here."

WESLEY'S WOBBLY WAGON WHEEL

Wesley felt like whistling as he hurried along with his red wagon. When he reached the village store, he parked the wagon and stepped inside.

Mr. Kolb looked up in surprise. "Well, look who's here. Are you by yourself, Wesley?"

Wesley's blue eyes twinkled, and he grinned, showing the empty space where his front teeth were missing. "Yes, sir. Daddy is working on the late shift and Tammy is sick. Mommy can't take her out. So I came to get the groceries," he explained. Digging in his blue jeans pocket he handed the list of things Mother needed to Mr. Kolb.

"That's fine," smiled Mr. Kolb. "Your Daddy will be glad to hear about you helping your mother." Taking the list, he bustled about, getting the groceries. In a short time everything was in two big bags. Wesley felt quite grown-up as he pulled a twenty-dollar bill from his pocket and paid for the groceries.

"Thank you," smiled Mr. Kolb, as he handed him the change. Mr. Kolb helped Wesley carry the bags outside and put them onto the wagon. "That's quite a load for you to take up the hill, but you'll make it," he said, chuckling.

The wagon didn't go as easily now as it had. Wesley noticed that one back wheel wobbled from side to side. He stopped and pushed it with his foot. It seemed all right, and he trudged right along to Jack and Bobby's house.

"Come in and play with us for a while," called Jack.

Wesley took off his cap and scratched his head. "I'd like to," he said. "But Mommy needs milk for Tammy's formula. I'll have to go right on home."

His arms grew tired of pulling the wagon, and he felt hot and sticky in spite of the nippy fall breeze. The back wheel kept wobbling, and the wagon seemed to pull harder and harder. He unzipped his jacket, leaned forward and pulled harder.

Suddenly, *bump, scra-a-pe.* Wesley looked back. His mouth fell open. Dropping the wagon tongue, he dashed back to rescue the groceries spilling out of the bags. The wobbly wagon wheel was rolling down the hill, pursued by oranges, a head of cabbage, and two cans of Tammy's milk.

Wesley lifted the corner of the wagon to stop the flow of groceries. As soon as he let go, it dropped down and more groceries fell out. Steadying the wagon with one hand, he managed to set the bags off on the sidewalk. Then he ran down the hill to collect the wheel and the scattered groceries. After several trips he had everything back in the bags.

Squatting down, Wesley looked at the wheel. The shiny hubcap was in its place. He couldn't see a thing wrong with it. He put the wheel back on the axle, set the bags on the wagon, and started up the hill again.

Everything seemed to be going along fine, until suddenly the back corner of the wagon dropped down again, and, once more, the wheel rolled down the hill. Wesley grabbed the back end of the wagon and lifted it just in time to keep the groceries from spilling.

He looked at the place were the wheel was supposed to be. He looked the wheel over again. It was new and shiny and looked perfectly all right to him.

Wesley looked up and down the hill trying to decide what to do. He was thinking of calling Jack and Bobby to come and help him when he saw their family zooming away in their new car. He thought of leaving everything there and running home to get Mother. But he remembered Mother warning him to stay right with the wagon so that no dogs would get the food.

Wesley sat right down on the sidewalk with

his chin in his hands. He simply could not carry everything. It was all that he could do to lift the bags into the wagon. How he wished Daddy or some man would come along to help him.

Suddenly a kind voice said, "Are you having trouble, Wesley?"

Wesley jumped and dabbed at the tears in the corners of his eyes as he looked up into his Sunday school teacher's smiling face. "Y . . . yes," he stammered. "My wagon wheel won't stay on, and I can't get the groceries home." To himself he thought, *I wish a man had come along. Miss Brown is a good Sunday school teacher, but what can she do about a wagon wheel that won't stay on?*

Miss Brown put her finger on her cheek as though she was thinking. Then she stooped down by Wesley and looked at the wheel, then at the wagon. "You lost a pin," she explained.

Opening her purse she took a nail file and began prying the shiny hubcap off the wheel. Wesley watched silently, not sure whether he liked what she was doing. After several tries the cap came off, and she laid it into the wagon.

Carefully she slid the wheel back onto the axle. "Now we need a pin," she said. "You don't happen to have a nail in your pocket, do you?"

Wesley thrust both hands deep into his pockets. "No, Ma'am," he shook his head sorrowfully.

Miss Brown's blue eyes twinkled. "Never mind," she smiled. Reaching up into her blond hair, she got a bobby pin. Wesley watched open-mouthed as she pried it wide open and slipped it through the tiny hole in the axle. Bending it around so that it could not slip out she smiled at Wesley. "There," she exclaimed, "it's not a very neat job, but it will keep your wheel on till your daddy can fix it."

Wesley's big blue eyes sparkled. "Thank you. Thank you," he cried.

The sun was slipping behind the mountains as he turned in at his own gate. Mother was at the door to meet him. "Oh, good. Here you are. I was getting concerned about you."

Wesley's face beamed as he told her about the lost wheel. "I knew Miss Brown was a good Sunday school teacher, but I didn't think she'd know anything about wagon wheels," he chuckled.

THE GREAT SURPRISE

Mother scraped the last rich, black soil into a flowerpot and glanced at the bulbs she needed to repot. Turning toward the lawn, she called, "Stanley, Judy, come here, please."

Stanley and Judy dropped their shovels into the sandpile and raced to the house to see what Mother wanted.

"I need more rich soil from the woods to finish repotting my flowers," said Mother as she placed a bulb into a pot. "Please take the wagon up along the creek where we got soil yesterday, and fill the buckets that are on the wagon."

Judy's eyes grew big. "Do you mean we can go all by ourselves?" she asked in surprise.

"Yes," Mother smiled. "You helped me so well yesterday. I'm sure you can do it yourselves. Then I can go right ahead with my planting."

Stanley's brown eyes sparkled. "That will

be fun," he exclaimed. "Come on, Judy. Let's go."

The children got Mother's shovel and hop-skipped to the wagon. With Stanley pulling and Judy trotting beside the wagon, they went out the walk and through the gate and the barnyard. Taffy, their golden collie, dashed up behind them just as they came to the gate leading through the orchard to the woods. His tail wagged eagerly, and he cocked his head to one side. "Can I come too?" his friendly eyes seemed to be saying.

Stanley patted Taffy's head and rubbed his ears. "Sure thing, Taffy, come along. You can help us," he said.

Taffy didn't wait for a second invitation. He ran ahead with his nose to the ground, sniffing as he went. Soon he bounded after a rabbit that dashed from a clump of grass beside the path. Mr. Rabbit ran so fast that Taffy gave up the chase and came panting back to the children with his tongue hanging out.

Soon the children were in the woods. It was cool in the shade, and the creek sang merrily as it hurried over rocks and down the hill toward the barn. Judy walked close to Stanley now. The long shadows of the trees made her nervous when Mother was not with them. She jumped when a squirrel ran across the path and scampered up a tree. Taffy stood at the foot of the tree and barked at the squirrel.

When they came to a large bed of ferns and

some lovely green moss, they knew they were close to the spot where Mother had gotten soil the day before. Yes, there it was, right behind a rotting log. After they filled the buckets, Judy helped Stanley set them up onto the wagon.

While they worked, Taffy darted here and there sniffing at tracks. Suddenly he gave a short bark and bounded away through the ferns and between some evergreens. "Bow-wow, bow-wow-wow, woof!" Taffy was excited.

"He must have something," exclaimed Stanley. "Let's go see what it is."

The children ran toward the sound of Taffy's barking. Just as they came in sight of the dog, he sniffed at a gray animal, gave it a shove with his nose, and stalked off with his tail between his legs. Stanley and Judy hurried up to see the animal. It lay on its back, perfectly still.

"What is it?" asked Judy.

"I don't know," Stanley admitted. "It looks like a rat, but it's too big. Anyhow, Taffy's a bad dog. He killed it."

"Let's take it along home and ask Mother what it is," suggested Judy. "Won't she be surprised if we bring an animal along?"

"I guess she will be surprised," chuckled Stanley. Slowly and carefully he picked the animal up by its long skinny tail and carried it over to the waiting wagon. It was heavier now, and both children pulled as they hurried home. The little animal lay still. Taffy had smelled another track and was so busy investigating, that he did not follow the children home.

When they came into their own yard, they dropped the wagon handle and dashed into the kitchen. "Mother, Mother, come and see what Taffy caught," they said in one breath.

Mother pushed back her brown hair, dusted the dirt off her hands, and followed the children outside. Stanley reached the wagon first. His mouth fell open. He couldn't believe his eyes. "It's gone!" he cried. "Where did it get to?"

"Look! Look!" shouted Judy, pointing toward the chicken house. There, shuffling along as fast as his legs would take him, went the gray animal. He wasn't even limping! Just as Taffy dashed into the barnyard, the little animal dived under the chicken house where no one could touch him. Taffy stood at the hole where the animal had disappeared and barked and barked and barked.

Mother smiled. "Well, well, Taffy, did you let the opossum play a trick on you?" she asked. "Even you thought he was dead." Turning to the children she explained. "That little animal is an opossum. God has given them the ability to act dead when they become badly frightened. You see, even Taffy thought the opossum was dead and let him alone. We say they are 'playing possum'."

"Is that why you say we are 'playing possum' when we pretend to be sleeping?" asked

Stanley, thrusting his hands deep into his pockets.

"That's right," answered Mother.

Stanley brushed some dirt off his denim trousers. "That was a good joke on us," he laughed. "We thought we were really going to surprise you, but Mr. Opossum surprised us!"

"And the opossum got a free ride on the wagon," added Judy.

JUST PRETENDING

Daddy drove up to the lawn gate and tapped on the horn. "Come quickly, Gregg, or we will be late for your appointment," he called.

Brent and Gail dropped their shovels into the sandbox and ran over to the station wagon. "May we go along?" they asked in one breath.

"Not today," Daddy answered. "Maybe you can go along this evening to deliver the freight I'm picking up for Uncle Jim."

"Just because Gregg is bigger than we are, he always gets to go along, and we have to stay at home," grumbled Brent.

Gail's pretty blue eyes clouded. "I know," she agreed. "It isn't fair."

Just then Brent's blue eyes lighted up. "Say, let's pretend we're going to the city and ride out the lane on our bikes," he said, as he ran to get his shiny, red tricycle.

"That will be fun," agreed Gail, bouncing

onto her shiny blue tricycle. Together they rode out the gate and up the hill, forgetting all about the rule that they were not permitted to go beyond the big maple tree beside the lane. It was hard pedaling up the hill on the bumpy lane. Gail's short legs grew tired. Brent's face got red and his shirttail came out of his trousers.

At the top of the hill, they stopped to rest. Grandma's house peeped between the trees at the foot of the lane across the highway. Gail's eyes sparkled. "Let's ride down to Grandma's house and pretend her nice smooth drive is the city," she suggested.

"Sure thing," agreed Brent. Away they went *bumpity, bumpity, bump, bump* down the lane, across the highway, and onto Grandma's drive. Round and round they drove, up one side and down the other. Gail's blond pigtails stood out in the breeze. "Whee, this is fun," she squealed.

At home, Mother fed Sandra and Sonja, the twins, and tucked them into their cribs. Then she went to the door to see what Gail and Brent were doing. They were nowhere in sight.

"Children," she called, "where are you?"

There was no answer. She cupped her hands around her mouth and called, "Gail! Brent! Yoo hoo, where are you?" Still there was no answer.

A puzzled look crossed Mother's face. She hurried out to the barn and called and called again and again. No answer. Swiftly she walked back to the house and tried to phone Grandma. There was no answer. Then she remembered that this was sewing day, and Grandma always went to the sewing. Mother was worried. She walked to the window and looked out. Then she turned back to the telephone and dialed a number.

"Hello, this is Mrs. Miller. I'm awfully sorry to bother you, Mrs. Blake," she apologized, "but Brent and Gail have disappeared. I'm here alone and don't have the car to go and look for them. Would you mind looking to see whether they may be over at my mother's house?"

"Just a minute, I'll check," answered Mrs. Blake. In a minute she was back. "Yes, they're over there riding their tricycles on the drive," she reported. "Now don't fret. I'll go over there and bring them home," she offered.

"Oh, thank you. I'll be so grateful if you do," answered Mother.

Soon Mrs. Blake drove up to the yard gate. Tears shimmered in Mother's eyes when she came out to thank Mrs. Blake for bringing the children home.

"You're quite welcome," said Mrs. Blake. Then she added, "If they were my children, I'd give them good, sound spankings."

Taking firm holds on the children's hands, Mother marched them into the house. She hugged them close and in a choky voice said, "Thank God you are safe. Now tell me why you went to Grandma's without permission?"

Brent's eyes blinked, and he looked down at the floor. Gail's eyes blinked, and she toyed with her pigtails. "We . . . we were just pretending to go to the city like Gregg and Daddy did," stammered Brent.

Mother's face was sober. "You gave me a terrible fright," she said. "Some pretend games are all right, but when they make you break rules and disobey, they are all wrong. Come with me. We will have to do something to help you remember to obey rules."

Leading the children to the utility room, Mother told them to sit on an old bench with no back. Then she went to get the baby gate out of storage, fastened it on the hinges and closed it tightly. "Now we will pretend that you have trespassed a law and will have to stay in prison until supper time," she explained. "I will be the jail keeper. Now I must do the ironing. So please do not bother me."

Gail and Brent looked at each other, glad that they escaped the spanking Mrs. Blake had recommended. But there were no toys in the playroom, and they soon tired of just sitting in jail. After a while Brent was thirsty and started to open the gate.

Mother gave his hand a sharp rap. "Stop tampering with the lock, or I will have to put handcuffs on you," she announced.

Brent's eyes grew big. "I . . . I just wanted to get a drink," he stammered.

"Don't tamper with the lock," Mother

repeated.

Soon Gail called, "I'm hungry, Mother; may I have a cookie, please?"

"Oh, no," exclaimed Mother. "In jail you eat only at mealtime."

Daddy and Gregg were surprised to find Gail and Brent in their utility-room prison. "Why . . . , what's happened?" Daddy asked.

"Tell Daddy why you are in jail," prompted Mother soberly.

Gail smoothed down her yellow dress. Brent rumpled his blond hair into a haystack. Slowly the just-pretending story came out.

"Well, well," said Daddy. "Prison is the right place for you under these circumstances."

"May we go along to take the freight over to Uncle Jim's?" asked Brent.

Daddy scratched his head. "You remember I said maybe you can go along. Do you think you deserve to go along after frightening Mother so badly?"

Gail and Brent dabbed at the tears that slipped from their eyes and rolled down their flushed cheeks. They slowly shook their heads.

"I'll stay home and play with them," Gregg offered sympathetically.

"You may visit the prisoners through the gate, but you cannot go into their cell," said Mother.

When Mother opened the gate, she hugged Gail and Brent close. "I'm so thankful my runaways are safe," she said. "And I'm sure they will remember not to pretend so much that it makes them disobey."

"We will," agreed Gail and Brent, nodding soberly.

MICHAEL'S NEW BOOK

Michael's eyes raced across the pages of the exciting, new animal book Uncle John had given him for his birthday.

Mother glanced at the clock. "Are you ready for school, Mike?" she asked. "The bus is due in five minutes."

"I want to finish this story," Mike answered.

"You had better come or you will have to *schussle* to get ready," Mother reminded him.

Michael frowned. He liked to hear his parents talk Pennsylvania German sometimes. He even liked to try to talk it himself sometimes. But he did not like the word *schussle.* Daddy called him *Schussle Mike* when he hurried through a job and didn't do it well.

Mike's thoughts slowed his reading. Suddenly he dropped the book and rushed to the sink to brush his teeth.

Screech, the bus came to a stop. Mike grabbed a comb and ran it through his hair twice, leaving some blue blanket fuzz in the back. Jerking the closet door open, he rammed one arm into his navy blue jacket, and then dashed for his lunch pail. His dangling jacket sleeve knocked Jimmy's block house down. "Mike, you *schussle-schussle Mike!*" Jimmy shouted angrily.

Mike ran for the front door, bumping into baby Sally, who was just learning to walk. Sally sat down hard and began crying loudly.

As Mike's legs flew toward the bus, Sally's cry and Jimmy's *schussle Mike,* rang in his ears. The bus seemed to make a song of *schussle Mike* and the gears sounded like Sally crying.

The tune kept ringing in his ears so that Mike couldn't do his lessons well that day. Not once until he was playing ball at recess could he forget it.

At home Mother dried her hands on her apron, picked up Sally and comforted her. With a sigh she also picked up the heap of clothes that had come down when Mike grabbed his jacket. She closed the closet door and turned tight the dripping faucets in the bathroom. Then she went back to her dish-washing.

"I wish Mike wouldn't be such a *schussle.* He knocked my house down," Jimmy complained.

Sally toddled into the playroom. She cooed with delight when she saw Mike's new book lying open, facedown on the couch. For a long time she sat on the floor, carefully paging and looking at pictures. She didn't know these were wild animals. She said, "Kitty, kitty," to the bobcat. She said, "Bow wow, bow wow," to the wolf, and "Moo, moo," to the moose. Then she happened to tear a page. *Rr-r-r-i-i-p*. The sound amused her. She tore another and giggled. By and by she tore the pretty red cover off. The book didn't look right now, so Sally toddled out to Mother and held it up for her to see. "Now, now, now," she said.

Mother gasped. She took the book and tried to fit the cover back on. It needed more attention than she had time to give it, so she laid it up on the cupboard out of Sally's reach. "I'll leave it there until Mike comes home," she said.

On the way home from school, Mike told his chums about his new, wild animal book. "I'll finish reading it tonight and bring it to school tomorrow for you to see," he promised.

Bang! went the door when Mike came home. He pitched his coat on a chair in the kitchen.

"Where's my book?" he demanded.

Mother took the book from the cupboard and handed it to Mike. "I'm sorry, Mike, but you left your book where Sally got it," she said.

Mike's eyes grew dark and stormy. "Oh! Oh! My new book! Why didn't you take it away from Sally? She's a bad, bad girl. You shouldn't let her have my things!" he exclaimed.

Mother laid her hand gently on Mike's shoulder and said, "Michael, I didn't know Sally had your book until she brought it to me. If you had put it on the shelf this morning, she would not have gotten it."

Mike shrugged away and began to scold again. "Well, why didn't you put it away before she got it?" he asked. "I promised Bob and Billy I'd bring it to school tomorrow, but now it's ruined."

Mother sighed. "I know you feel bad about it, Mike, and I am sorry. Perhaps you had better take the book to your room and think this over. You can buy a new one with your savings or fix this one with tape and glue."

Mike rumpled his red hair so that it stood up like a haystack. Then he stomped up to his room. Banging the door behind him, he slouched down on his bed and tried to straighten up the book. "Why doesn't Mother take care of my things when I'm in school? What will I tell Bob and Bill when I show them the book?" he complained aloud.

At last he had every page and the cover in its proper place. While he was working, he had been thinking too. "I guess it really was my fault," he finally admitted to himself. "I should have been ready this morning when the bus came. Then I wouldn't have upset Jimmy's block house or Sally, and I wouldn't have forgotten to put my book away." He knelt down beside his bed and asked God to forgive him and to help him not to be a *schussle* Mike.

"I'll tell Bob and Bill the truth," he decided. Feeling much better, he went downstairs to where Mother was working in the kitchen. He stood watching her for a few minutes, and then he cleared his throat. "I'm sorry I was cross, Mother," he said. "I've fixed up the book, and I'm going to keep it to remind me not to be a *schussle* Mike. After this I'll get ready for school, then if there's any time left, I'll read until the bus comes."

And he did.

STRANDED IN THE MOUNTAINS

Daddy drove slowly along the winding mountain road. In the distance a rosy sunset glowed beyond evergreens loaded with snow.

Karen's brown eyes sparkled, and her cheeks glowed in the reflection of the sunset. "Oh! How beautiful!" she gasped. "It looks like a picture."

"It does," Daddy agreed. "I'm glad we took this shortcut road across the mountains. All this scenery is worth some bumps."

Just then a shrill "Sqea . . . eee . . . eek," followed by a "rattle, thump, bump," startled them all.

Daddy stopped the car quickly and got out. He lifted the hood and then announced, "The fan belt is torn. Now I wish we were out on the highway. It's hard to tell when someone will come along here."

"What will we do now?" asked Dale.

Daddy climbed back into the car. "We can't go on without a fan belt, that's for sure. It would ruin the motor."

"But, Daddy, you said we'd get home in time for Sunday school tomorrow," Karen said anxiously.

"I'll have to walk ahead and get help," Daddy decided.

Karen looked at the fast-fading daylight. "Please don't go. It's getting dark," she begged.

"Mother will stay with you," Daddy assured her. Opening the car door, he paused and listened. "I believe somebody's coming," he said. Sure enough! Dim lights appeared around the bend. An old, old car came chugging up beside them and blew the horn. "Ger . . . ooga, ooga, ooga." Karen and Dale burst out laughing at the funny sound.

Then the car stopped and a kind voice called, "Need help, mister?"

"Yes, sir," Daddy answered. "Our fan belt's torn and we're miles from home. How far is it to a garage?"

The man cleared his throat. "About 40 miles, and it's closed over the weekend," he answered slowly. Then his face brightened. "My name's George, Paul George. My wife and I will be glad to put you up over Sunday. It's sort of lonesome on the farm since all our children have gone."

Karen leaned across Mother's shoulder.

"Let's take the bus home. I want to be in Sunday school tomorrow."

"Sorry, sister," said Mr. George. "No buses run through here."

Daddy looked at Mother. Mother looked at Daddy. "Thank you, Mr. George. We'll accept your offer."

In a short time Daddy had locked up the car, and the family was packed into Mr. George's old, old car. *Bumpity, bounce* down the mountain they chugged. Karen's head touched the ceiling when they hit a big bump. Every time they came to a turn, Mr. George blew the horn, "Ger . . . ooga, ooga."

"This is fun," shouted Dale.

"But we can't go to Sunday school tomorrow," Karen protested.

"We'll be glad to take you along to our mission Sunday school at the schoolhouse," said Mr. George. "You'll like Pastor Davis and his wife."

Karen leaned against Mother and wondered what Sunday school in a schoolhouse would be like.

Mrs. George flung the door of the neat, little farmhouse wide open and invited everyone in to the warmth of the kitchen stove. With Mother's help she soon prepared a good supper. It seemed strange to eat in the dim yellow light of kerosene lamps.

After supper the children went with Mr. George to see the animals. Karen thought the baby lambs were the cutest, but Dale like Leo, the dog, best of all.

The children's eyes sparkled, and their cheeks glowed when they came in. They watched, fascinated, as Mrs. George shook the ashes down into a small box at the bottom of the stove and added more coal to the fire.

At bedtime Mrs. George took a small oil lamp from the shelf and led the way up the narrow stairway to a room with two beds. The long shadows on the wall almost frightened Karen. The room was cold.

"Brr, I don't like this cold room." Karen's teeth chattered as she wiggled into her pajamas.

"Never mind," Mother assured her. "You will soon be warm under this mountain of covers."

When Karen awoke the next morning, Mother was lighting the oil lamp. After breakfast she snuggled against Mother and said, "Let's stay here. We don't have our Sunday clothes."

Mrs. George's kind blue eyes looked down at her. "Don't mind your clothes, honey," she smiled. "The blue dress you have on is all right."

Karen was surprised to see how neat and clean the schoolroom was. Waves of heat from the old, pot-bellied stove in the back warmed her and made her feel welcome. The children grinned shyly and invited her to come into their class. Still wondering what it was going to be like to have Sunday school in a schoolroom, Karen followed a little girl to a seat in the corner by the blackboard.

Karen's next surprise came when the children burst into happy singing. When everyone joined in the singing, it seemed like a larger group than her home Sunday school. Another surprise awaited her. Mrs. Davis taught the same lesson with the same materials and memory verses that Miss Miller used at home. She made the lesson so interesting that Karen forgot where she was. Before she could believe it, the bell rang and class was over.

Outside after Sunday school, Karen took hold of Mother's hand. "I liked this Sunday school. I'm glad we had to stay here. I'd like to come again sometime."

THE BEAUTIFUL BLUE MARBLE

Ivan tucked his blue shirt into his navy trousers and dropped to his knees on the rug. "It's my turn to have that beautiful blue marble first today," he announced.

"All right," agreed Becky, her brown eyes thoughtful. "But I'll shoot it first and put it at the end of my row where it's harder to get."

Ivan lined his marbles up with the blue one right in the middle of his row. Becky put a red one in the middle of her row.

"All right, you shoot first, Becky," Ivan said.

Becky dropped to her knees, tucking her dress under them, and tossed back her brown pigtails. Leaning far forward she aimed straight at the beautiful marble with her big green shooter. Oops, she missed it! "Oooh," she groaned. "That bump in the floor made me miss it."

Ivan aimed his big blue shooter at Becky's red marble. *Ping!* He hit it, and Becky rolled it over for him to add it to his marbles.

Now it was Becky's turn to shoot again. But try as she would, she couldn't hit her favorite blue marble. At last she managed to hit it, but Ivan hit it during his next turn and got it right back again.

Becky's eyes darkened as though the sun had hidden behind a cloud. Slowly she rolled it over to him and waited for him to put it in line. Carefully she aimed, squinted, and shot. *Ping.* The beautiful marble was hers once more.

"I can't let you have that beauty," declared Ivan, and once more, it was his.

Becky had to work a long time before she hit the pretty blue marble again. "Goody, goody!' she shouted. She picked up the beauty, admiring its flashing blue colors as she slowly turned it in her hands. "I'm glad I have you back," she told the marble, putting it up to her mouth and kissing it.

Suddenly an idea popped into her head. *I know what I'll do. I'll put it into my mouth for a while. That way Ivan can't take it from me right away again,* she decided. Into Becky's mouth went the prized marble.

A frown spread over Ivan's face and his dark eyes snapped. "Hey, that's not fair," he protested.

"You had it much more than I did," Becky mumbled past the marble in her mouth. "Let me keep it till you hit the fourth one of my other marbles. Then I will put it back in line again," she coaxed.

Ivan rumpled his thick black hair, "All right," he agreed. "But remember. The minute I hit four of yours, back into the line it goes." He had soon hit three. On his fourth turn he squinted and aimed very carefully but missed badly.

Becky giggled. Then it happened! Suddenly the marble was not in her mouth. It was slipping down her throat. And there it stuck! Becky couldn't get it up. She couldn't get it down. She couldn't talk. Worse yet, she couldn't breathe!

Running to Ivan she pointed to her mouth and made strange gasping sounds.

"Mother! Mother! Come quick! Becky's choking," he shouted.

Mother came dashing from the kitchen. When she saw Becky's blue lips, her own face turned white. She grabbed Becky, turned her upside down over her knee and slapped her back hard between her shoulders. Becky squirmed, kicked, and thrashed about. She wanted to cry, but no sound came. She wanted to tell Mother that she thought the marble was moving on down now, but she couldn't talk.

In spite of her nurses' training Mother was trembling. She shook and pounded until she was weak, then she turned Becky upright and saw that her face was not as blue anymore. Tears were streaming down her cheeks. She was swallowing hard over and over. Her breath was coming in great gasps. At last she stammered, "It . . . w . . . w . . .went down!"

"Thank God!" exclaimed Mother. Becky breathed hard and sobbed, just leaning against Mother for a long time.

Ivan looked on with frightened eyes. "She put that pretty blue marble into her mouth so that I wouldn't get it," he explained.

Becky sobbed harder. "Now it's gone. I wish I had let you have it. What'll happen to me, Mother?"

Mother drew Becky close. "Don't cry about the marble, Becky. Thank God that it went on down, and you didn't choke. I think you will be fine. Marbles are round and have no sharp edges. If it gets down to your stomach, it shouldn't cause any problems. I'll ask Dr. Glass, but I'm sure there's nothing to worry about. I'm also sure you have learned a lesson on selfishness you will never forget."

Becky looked up through teary eyes. "Yes, Mother, I did. I'm sorry I was so selfish, Ivan. I'll never, never put anything in my mouth again to keep you from getting it!"

LEFT BEHIND

It was Sunday evening and almost church time when Alton came bounding into the kitchen. "Daddy, the right front tire on the station wagon is flat," he announced.

"Hmmm," said Daddy. "The spare tire is low in air, and we won't have time to change it. I'll call Grandpa Bender and see if some of you children can go to church with them. The rest of us can squeeze into the VW."

"It's time for everybody to get ready for church right now. Remember, the missionary family from Japan will be there tonight," added Mother. Taking Willy by the hand, she led him to the bathroom to wash the chocolate ice cream off his face.

Larry and Linda were putting a puzzle together. Linda dropped the piece she had and ran to get ready. Larry glanced at baby Patty still sleeping in her bassinette. "Patty isn't ready yet. I can put these last few pieces into my puzzle and still be ready in time," he told himself.

Just as he completed the bear's nose, Mother came into the room. "Larry Brunk!" she exclaimed. "You go and get ready this minute. We don't want to be late for church."

Larry jumped and scurried upstairs. On his way up, he met the little and middle-sized Brunks on their way down in their go-to-church clothes.

Mother, with Patty in her arms, stepped outside just as Grandpa and Grandma drove in to pick up some of the children. "If it's all right with you, the children can sit with us in church," called Grandma.

"All right," replied Mother. "We will be coming soon."

Daddy picked up Willy and paused on the porch. "Everybody out?" he called. Nobody answered. Daddy turned the key in the lock and walked to the car.

Larry was sloshing water over his face in the bathroom and didn't hear Daddy. He dived into his blue trousers, stuck his feet in his black shoes, and dashed down the stairs. Just as he reached the bottom step, he saw the car pulling out of the drive onto the road.

"Wait! Wait!" he shouted. He ran to the door and grabbed the knob. It wouldn't turn. It was locked, and Daddy had the key in his pocket. By the time he got to the window, Daddy and Mother were driving down the highway.

Larry ran back to the door. He yanked on the knob and kicked the door. It was no use; the door wouldn't budge. He raced to the back door. It was locked too.

Tears flowed from Larry's eyes, rolled down his flushed cheeks, and landed on his clean white shirt. "They're gone. They went without me. And it will soon be dark," he said aloud. He seemed to hear his heart thump the words in his head.

He pitched himself facedown on the couch and cried so loudly that Sport, the dog, began to howl in sympathy outside on the porch. The louder Larry cried, the louder Sport howled.

By and by Larry tried to stop crying. He sat up, sniffled, and wiped his nose and eyes on his white shirtsleeve. Then he spied the candy dish with the lollipops Daddy had brought home yesterday. "Maybe it won't seem so long if I suck a lollipop. Mother and Daddy won't mind if I eat a second one today since I'm all alone," he reasoned.

Larry chose a red lollipop and popped it into his mouth. It did make his throat feel better. He walked to the playroom and saw the neatly finished bear puzzle. He gave it a shove, scattering pieces all over the table. "If I'd only dropped you and gone to get ready when Mother told me to, I wouldn't be here alone," he told the bear.

Just then Sport growled, dashed down off the porch, and barked savagely. Larry's knees shook and his chin quivered. He crouched down onto the floor. *Suppose a robber comes and finds me all alone,* he thought.

Then he noticed the Bible school books on the bottom shelf of the bookcase. He pulled some out and began to page through them. "Here are some of the verses I learned in Bible school," he told himself. "I'm going to see if I can remember them when I look at the pictures."

The first one he remembered made him hang his head. "Children, obey your parents," he read. "If I would have obeyed Mother, I could be listening to the missionary from Japan right now," he said and sighed deeply.

Larry paged on. "I remember this one. 'God is my helper.' I really need a helper now." Quickly he bowed his head and clasped his hands. "Dear Jesus, be my helper. I'm all alone," he prayed. The next verse he recognized was, "I will trust and not be afraid."

"I do feel better now since I prayed. God is helping me not to be afraid," he assured himself.

Larry got up and carried all the books to the table where he could spread them out to look at.

In church the missionary's wife invited the children up for children's meeting. When the missionaries' little girls stood to sing "Jesus Loves Me" in Japanese, all the boys and girls leaned forward to listen. That is, all except one little girl. Linda turned and looked back at

Mother. She didn't seem to hear the singing girls. Her chin began to quiver, and tears rolled down her rosy cheeks.

Daddy looked puzzled and signaled for her to come back to him.

As Linda went, she put her arm up over her forehead to hide her tears. Daddy picked up Willy so that he wouldn't wiggle. Stepping out to the aisle, Daddy led Linda outside. "What's wrong, honey?" he asked.

"Where's Larry?" sobbed Linda.

Daddy's mouth fell open. "Didn't he come with Grandpas?"

"No, he wasn't ready."

Daddy rubbed his chin thoughtfully. "We can't leave a six-year-old at home alone," he said. "I'll go get him right away. You slip in quietly and tell Mother I'm going after Larry."

Inside, Mother was finding it hard to keep her mind on the singing. She was wondering what Linda's trouble was. She glanced over at the row of boys and girls. There was Ella with her arm around Johnny who had just started going to children's meeting. Alton and Danny were sitting with friends. But where was Larry?

Just then Linda slipped in beside Mother and whispered that Daddy had gone to get Larry. Sudden tears shimmered in Mother's eyes. Linda scooted tight against her. Shifting Patty on her lap, Mother laid her arm across Linda's shoulder to let her know she could stay with her if she didn't feel like going back to children's meeting without her twin.

Larry was paging through the last Bible school book when Daddy came bounding up onto the porch with Willy in one arm. He set Willy down and unlocked the door. Larry flew into his daddy's arms and snuggled against him with a sob. "I'm sorry we missed taking you along, Larry," said Daddy. "We thought you went with Grandpas."

"I'm sorry I didn't go get ready when Mother told me to," Larry sobbed. Daddy helped Larry wash away the tear and lollipop stains, and they drove the seven miles back to church. By the time they got there, children's meeting was over. Larry sat very quietly between Daddy and Mother and listened to the message.

After services when Daddy walked by a group of little boys playing in the parking lot, he called, "Come, boys, it's time to go home." Can you guess who stopped chasing other boys and raced for the car?

MARGIE'S GIFT

Margie ripped the wrapping paper off her birthday gift from Aunt Kate and peeked inside the box. A cloud of disappointment spread over her face. All she could see were two brown somethings. Then she spied a note in the bottom of the box.

Picking it up, she read, "Dear little flower lover: These are narcissus bulbs. Plant them as soon as the instructions say, and they should bloom sometime in April. I know you will take good care of them, and I hope to enjoy some of their good smell when I come home for spring vacation. With love, Aunt Kate."

Margie's sunny smile bounced back into place, and her blue eyes sparkled. Picking up the brown bulbs, she hurried to the kitchen to show them to Mother.

Mother smiled. "There are flowerpots and soil in the basement," she said. "Shall we go down and pot them now?"

Margie and Mother went downstairs. Working together, they soon had the bulbs planted. Then Margie carried the pot upstairs and set it in a sunny, living room window. Every day Margie looked at the pot. One morning the brown soil was raised into a little hill at one spot. Margie looked closely. "Mother! Mother," she called, "come and see what's happening."

"I see," said Mother when Margie showed her the bump of soil in the pot. "Soon you will see a green shoot coming up from that little hill."

Mother was right. The very next day a green tip began to show. And it wasn't long until two plants were pushing right out of the brown soil. Margie watered them carefully and they grew and grew. By mid-April several plump green buds had appeared.

Margie skipped down the steps and out to the street to join her best friend, Jane, on her way to school. "Oh, Jane," she exclaimed. "My narcissus buds are coming out. You must come to see the first one that opens."

"I will. I will," replied Jane. "I just love to smell narcissus."

Every day Margie could see that the buds were growing fatter. White began to show along the tips, and Jane stopped in to see if she couldn't get a whiff of their sweet smell. But they only smelled green.

One Thursday morning, Margie was waiting to walk to school with Jane. But Jane didn't come. Finally Margie had to go on alone or be late for school. She was puzzled. When she got to school, she saw a group of children gathering around Miss Martin, the teacher.

"Yes, she slipped on the ice in front of her home just this morning. Her leg is broken, and she will need to be in the hospital for several weeks," Margie heard Miss Martin say.

Whom were they talking about? *Surely it can't be Jane,* thought Margie. But it was Jane. A big lump came into Margie's throat, almost choking her. All during the day, Margie kept thinking of Jane and wishing she could do something for her.

On Friday morning a sweet fragrance greeted Margie when she stepped into the living room. Three of the pretty white flowers were opening.

Suddenly Margie thought of Jane lying in the hospital. She was sad that Jane could not come see the narcissus in bloom. For a minute Margie held her chin in her hand and stared at the narcissus. Then she had an idea.

Quickly she turned and hurried to the kitchen. "Mother, the narcissus buds are opening. Could I take them to Jane in the hospital?" she asked.

Mother smiled. "That would be a fine idea," she agreed.

Margie went back to the window and stooped to get a good full breath of sweet-smelling flowers. *Oh, it's going to be hard to give them up,* she thought. *And what will Aunt*

Kate think? Maybe she won't like it if I give my gift to someone else. But Margie went to find some pretty paper to wrap the plant in to protect it from the cold wind.

That afternoon, right after school, Mother and Margie went to see Jane at the hospital. It made Margie feel good to see how happy Jane was when she saw the flowers and sniffed the sweet narcissus odor.

That evening when Aunt Kate arrived, Margie noticed that she seemed to be looking for the flowers. Margie tossed back her brown pigtails and cleared her throat. "I-I hope you don't mind," she began, "but my friend Jane fell and broke her leg and has to be in the hospital. So Mother and I took the narcissus in to the hospital for her to enjoy. I'm sorry you won't get to smell them now."

A big smile crossed Aunt Kate's face. She drew Margie close and gave her a big hug. "Never mind about me not getting to smell the flowers," she said. "Knowing that you are an unselfish little girl is better than smelling the flowers could be. I'm glad Jane can enjoy them."

Margie's face beamed, and she felt happy from head to toe.

MISTER BUMP

This is a true story about a childhood experience of the author's.

Rhoda yawned two big yawns. She watched Grandmother's knitting needles flashing in and out of the pretty pink yarn. "When do you think Daddy and Mother will come for me?" she asked.

Grandmother glanced at the clock. "I think they'll be here before long," she said, smiling.

"I thought they'd be here before now. Maybe something happened to them," Rhoda's chin began to quiver.

Grandmother looked up from the sweater she was knitting to see a big tear splash down on Rhoda's blue dress. Laying her knitting aside, she brushed the brown hair back from Rhoda's face. She put her arm around Rhoda and drew her closer to her on the couch. "I don't think so, dear. I'm sure they're all right.

We know Jesus is taking care of them. Shall I tell you a story while we wait?"

Rhoda's blue eyes lit up. "Yes, please do. Tell me a story about when you were a little girl."

Grandmother's eyes were thoughtful as she picked up her knitting again. "I'll tell you about the long wait my brother and I had when Mr. Bump chased us."

Rhoda sat up straight. "Who was Mr. Bump?" she asked.

"He was my father's cross, old sheep," Grandmother explained. "He got his name because he seemed to think he should bump anybody who came near the flock of sheep.

"My father had warned my brother and me to stay out of the sheep pasture. But one spring afternoon we wanted some excitement. So we decided to go see Mr. Bump."

"Weren't you afraid?" Rhoda asked.

"Yes, I was," Grandmother admitted. "But my older brother, Ivan, said the walk would be fun, and we wouldn't go close to Mr. Bump. So we slipped through the gate and followed the path through the orchard, up beyond the lime quarry. We saw squirrels scampering up trees. A skinny woodchuck, just awakened from his winter sleep, was looking for something to eat. Two rabbits raced each other across the grass. We were so busy watching everything that we forgot to be careful.

"Before we knew it, we were right among the sheep. Mr. Bump jerked up his head, stamped his feet, and started right for us!

" 'Quick!' cried Ivan. He grabbed my hand and helped me up a steep bank of earth and shale that had been put there by a steam shovel. We got out of Mr. Bump's reach just in the nick of time.

"He tried to follow us, but the loose earth kept sliding down with him. We threw shale and dirt down into his big, black face and shouted at him, hoping to drive him away. But it only made him more furious and determined to get us. He stayed right there, tossing his head and pawing the bank as though threatening what he would do if we came down."

"Why didn't you go to the top of the bank and down on the other side?" Rhoda asked.

"We couldn't," Grandmother explained. "There was only a gaping hole on the other side where limestone had been taken out. I was afraid to go near the top. And I was getting tired of sliding down and scrambling back up to keep out of Mr. Bump's reach. So I began to cry.

" 'Don't cry. Somebody will come after us,' Ivan tried to comfort me. He dug out hollows for us to sit in so that we didn't have to keep climbing to stay up.

"We waited and waited and waited. The sun began to sink behind the mountain. Ivan's face grew sober when he remembered that Father would think we were in the house, and Mother would think we were at the stable.

" 'Let's ask Jesus to help us,' he suggested. So we bowed our heads and told Jesus all about it and asked Him to send somebody to help us or make Mr. Bump go away."

"Did he send someone?" Rhoda asked.

"No. All we could do was sit there and wait. We called and called. But nobody heard us, and nobody came. My teeth began chattering. I was afraid we would have to stay there all night long. But Ivan reminded me of a memory verse I had learned. 'He careth for you.' Ivan explained that the verse meant that Jesus loves us and takes care of us.

"While we sat thinking about that, we heard father calling the sheep. 'Sheep, sheep, sheep,' we heard faintly from way down at the barn. The sheep heard it too. They knew Father's voice. And they trusted him to give them a safe shelter and food for the night.

"The mother sheep lifted their heads and said, 'Ba-r-rr, ba-r.'

" 'Sheep, sheep, sheep,' we heard Father call again. Snatching last bites of grass, the ewes trotted off with their lambs along the winding path and disappeared down over the hill.

"Mr. Bump baaed in his gruff voice when he saw his family leave. Still he stood there and shook his big head at us. The ewes answered his baa down over the hillside. Suddenly Mr. Bump turned and went bounding after them.

"Finally our long wait was ending. We waited only long enough to be sure he wouldn't come back. Then we scrambled down and followed as fast as our cramped legs would take us. Father had just closed the door to the sheep stable when we came home."

Rhoda had been listening so closely to the story that she didn't hear a car stop outside. "That was a good story," she sighed. "Jesus helped you even without sending someone."

Just then Daddy and Mother came in the front door. "Are you ready to go home, Rhoda?" Daddy asked.

Rhoda bounced down. "Yes, Daddy. I was getting sleepy and tired of waiting. But Grandma's good story made waiting easy."

SOMETHING BETTER TO DO

David's summer visitor, Tony, was riding David's training bike. "Beep, beep," said David, whizzing past him on a scooter.

"It's too bumpy here in the barnyard," complained Tony. "I can't go fast." He was thinking of the smooth pavements in his New York City home. "Let's go out on the highway, and we can really have some fun," he added.

David's blue eyes opened wide in surprise. "Oh, we can't do that. It wouldn't be safe. There's too much traffic."

"Traffic," said Tony. "You should come to New York. Then you would see what traffic is."

David thought a moment. It would be nice riding out there. But he remembered that Daddy had said, "Never play out on the highway. The steep hill with the curve makes it too dangerous."

"No," he said firmly. "Mother would not allow us to go out there. Cars come very fast around the curve and down the hill."

Just then Mother came out. "Mr. Collins just called from the post office to say that our broiler chicks are there," she said.

"Oh, may we go along to get them?" asked David.

"I'm sorry," said Mother, "but you know Daddy is away with the truck. I don't see how I could get twelve hundred chicks and two boys into the car."

"Couldn't we stand?" begged the boys.

"No, the car will be full," answered Mother firmly. "We weren't expecting the chicks today. I wish the fountains and feeders were filled already, but I will manage someway. You boys can play nicely out here. Grandma is resting in her bedroom. If you need her, you can call. But don't disturb her unless you must. She has a headache."

David opened the big gate for Mother. "Bye," she called. "I should be back within an hour."

"Now," said Tony, "here's our chance. We can go out there on the highway and have a swell time, and your mother will never know."

David's mouth fell open. What should he do? His mother trusted him. "I can't do that. I would know and God would know," he said. "I just can't disappoint my mother. I guess I love her too much."

"Huh, so you are Mommy's good little sissy,

are you?" asked Tony. "Why, in New York we play on the streets and our mothers don't say a word."

David didn't like to be a sissy, but what could he do?

Tony's black eyes snapped. "I'm going out there whether you are or not," he declared. Then shaking his fist at David, he said, "And if you tell your mother on me, I'll show you what happens to tattletales in New York."

What shall I do? thought David. *Maybe I could hold the gate shut. No, that wouldn't be the answer. Tony could go through the small gate. Besides, Tony might use his fists. Maybe I should call Grandmother. No, Mother said not to call her unless I have to. Besides, she couldn't stop him.*

By this time Tony was at the gate. Just then David thought of something Daddy had told him. "If you are tempted to do something wrong, ask God to show you something better to do."

Quickly David bowed his head, closed his eyes, and clasped his hands. "Dear God," he prayed, "help me stop Tony. And please show us something better to do."

A thought came to him. When he opened his eyes, a big trailer truck was whizzing by. Tony jumped and rubbed his leg.

"Tony," called David, "would you like to help me surprise Mother?"

"How?" asked Tony.

"Remember, she said she wasn't ready for

the chicks. We can put water in the fountains and feed in the feeders."

"Sure thing," agreed Tony. He drove the bike with training wheels into the lawn and parked it.

The boys filled a bucket with water and started toward the brooder house. Splash! It swished out on their bare feet. The water made little streams through the dust on their feet. "Woo, that's cold," said Tony, laughing, "but it feels good."

Tony filled feeders while David put water into the fountains.

"Now we will scatter some feed on these newspapers for the chicks to pick up until they find the feeders," David explained.

It wasn't long until Mother was home. "What a wonderful surprise," she said. "I thought I would have to leave the chicks in the boxes until we got these things done. Now who wants to help get the chicks out of the boxes and give each one a drink?"

"We do. We do!" shouted the boys. There was so much peeping they had to shout to hear each other.

Tony laughed when the little chicks flapped their wings and ran. "They act just like I felt when I came here where there is lots of room to play," he said.

It was fun to watch the little chicks picking at the feed on the newspapers and drinking water from the fountains. "I'm glad I don't have to put my head way back like that to take a drink," said Tony. "But they don't seem to mind. They sound happy now."

David showed Tony how to hold a wee yellow chick and cover him with his hand. Tony giggled. "Oh, it tickles," he said. The little chick peeped very softly and was soon fast asleep.

"He thinks he's under his mother's wings," explained David. "Now we had better go eat our lunch. I'm hungry," he added.

"This was really a fine morning," said Tony, smiling at David on the way to the house. "Say, what were you doing out there this morning when you had your eyes closed?" he asked.

"I was praying," answered David. "I asked God to stop you from going out on the highway and to show me something better for us to do."

"Well, He sure answered quickly!" exclaimed Tony. "I couldn't think what you were doing with your eyes closed. Then when that big truck went by, a piece of gravel flew up and hit my leg. Woo! Did that burn! I was glad I wasn't closer."

"Yes, God answered quickly," agreed David. "It made me think of a memory verse we learned in Sunday school. It said, 'While they are yet speaking, I will hear.' God helped me think of something good to do."

SOUNDS IN THE NIGHT

Jack closed the book he was reading and looked at Daddy. "Please, Daddy, may Bobby and I go camping as the boys in this story did?" he asked.

Daddy scratched his head. "Well, I think the boys in the story were older than you and Bobby are. You boys are rather young to sleep outside alone. You might get scared."

"Scared? Ha! What is there to be scared about? Nothing could scare me," Jack boasted.

"There's really no danger, of course," Daddy agreed. "But sometimes shadows look strange in the dark. Sometimes noises sound strange when you can't tell what makes them."

"Oh, I like the night sounds," Jack insisted.

"Please, let us," begged Bobby, hopping around on one foot.

"All right," said Daddy, "you may try sleeping out under the trees not too far away. Then you will not have far to come to the house if you want to."

"We won't come in before morning," declared Jack. "Come on, Bobby, let's get some blankets and go out right away."

The boys gathered up some blankets and a flashlight and made a bed under a big maple tree behind their home. Then they climbed into their bed.

"This is fun," whispered Jack, shifting to get off a stone that was hurting his back.

Soon it grew quite dark. The lights from the kitchen windows shone across the yard. The boys watched Mother walking across the kitchen. They both wished she would come to say good night, but of course, they didn't say so.

Then the boys heard something coming closer and closer. Jack hunted for the flashlight, his hands shaking. Before he could find it, something cold and wet touched his cheek. Jack jumped out of his blanket bed.

"Bow, wow! Bow wow!" the big something said.

"Oh, Jocko, you scared me," gasped Jack. Jocko wagged his stubby tail and curled up by the boys. He sighed a dog sigh and was soon fast asleep.

As the boys' eyes were closing, a cricket chirped right nearby, and suddenly, they were wide-awake again. They listened to the katydids. Some seemed to say, "Katy did," and some to say, "Katy didn't."

After awhile Bobby went to sleep, and Jack

felt more alone than ever. He tried to find a soft spot for his head. Then he heard big steps coming toward him, nearer and nearer. When he found the flashlight and pressed the button, no light came. His scalp tingled as though his hair were standing up. Sitting up straight, he grabbed Bobby's arm and shook him. Bobby only moaned in his sleep. As Jack scrambled to his feet, Daisy, the old cow, said, "Moo," loudly on the other side of the fence. Jack jumped, then dropped back down on his blanket bed. Daddy was right. *Sounds do sound strange in the night.*

Just as Jack was almost asleep, a terrible screech sounded nearby. Grabbing Bobby by the shoulders, Jack shook him awake. "Did you hear that awful noise, Bobby? Come on. Let's go to the house." Bobby's teeth chattered and he began to cry as he staggered to his feet. The boys stumbled toward the house. No friendly lights in the kitchen showed them the way.

On the porch the boys bumped into something. Daddy's kind voice said, "It's all right, boys. That was only a screech owl calling her mate."

Drawing the boys close, Daddy sat down on the steps and talked quietly to them until their racing hearts slowed down.

"Shall we go inside now, or would you like for me to come out and sleep with you under the trees?"

"Oh, please do come out and sleep with us,"

chorused the boys.

With a small hand in each of his strong hands, Daddy walked to the blankets under the maple tree. Snuggling down, one on each side of Daddy, the boys yawned sleepily.

Jack lay listening to the night sounds. Crickets chirped and katydids argued. Bullfrogs croaked, "Car-unk, car-unk," in the distance. There was a steady munching as Daisy grazed nearby. Suddenly the owl screeched again from the treetop.

Jack snuggled closer to Daddy. "I'm not afraid when you are here," he whispered. "Night sounds are friendly when I know what they are."

"That's right," agreed Daddy. "It helps to remember that God is our Father too, and He is always with us."

"Yes, and even when we don't know what the sounds are, God does," Bobby said.

"After this, when I get frightened I will try to think of the verse, 'I will trust and not be afraid,' " Jack added.

Soon the three were fast asleep under the maple tree.

MOTHER'S PRODIGAL BROTHER

Galen's blue eyes sparkled as he looked at Uncle Rick's shiny red motorcycle. He rubbed his hand over the soft cushioned seat. "Will you give me a ride, please?" he asked.

Uncle Rick's dark eyes snapped. Jerking his hands out of his dirty trouser pockets, he gave Galen a hard shove. "No!" he barked. "Now scram, and don't you touch my motorcycle."

Galen scrammed.

The next day when Galen heard Uncle Rick's motorcycle roaring up the road, he dropped his ball and started running toward the house. Uncle Rick turned into the drive and right onto the sidewalk, straight toward Galen. Screaming with fright, Galen sprinted up the steps.

On his way indoors, Rick pulled Tabby cat's tail so that she yowled with pain. He kicked

Pal, the dog, so that he yelped, tucked his tail between his legs, and dashed behind the house. Inside he plunked a book down on Galen's head with a thud and pulled his ears. He pulled Janet's red curls and snatched her toys to make her cry.

As the days went by, Janet became more and more afraid of Uncle Rick. She cried as soon as she caught sight of him. Galen learned to scram before Uncle Rick told him to.

Uncle Rick was mean. He looked scary too. His hair was long and unkempt. He had a straggly beard and a curved mustache. His clothes were dirty and smelly.

One Friday evening when Mother called the family to supper Rick slouched toward the table. Accidentally tripping over Janet's toy duck, he knocked his elbow against the wall. He swore angrily.

Janet began crying, even though she was in Mother's arms. Galen took a tight hold on her skirt.

With quick steps Daddy walked over and laid his hand on Rick's shoulder. "Rick," he said, gently but firmly, "as head of the house, I will not allow you to use profanity in my home!"

Uncle Rick shrugged away. "You're as bad as my dad. Don't even let a fellow express himself," he snapped. "I'm leaving." Without even a good-by, he grabbed his jacket, dashed outside, and roared off on his motorcycle.

Galen was startled when Mother burst into

tears and went to her room. Supper grew cold on the table. No one felt like eating.

That night, and every night afterwards, Mother and Daddy prayed for Rick. "Uncle Rick is bad. Why do you ask God to bless him?" Galen wanted to know.

Daddy cleared his throat and crossed his long legs. "Yes," he agreed, "some of the things Uncle Rick does are bad. This makes us sad, but we still love him. God loves him too, and wants Uncle Rick to become His child."

Three months passed. One day Daddy brought in the mail and handed it to Mother. "There's a letter from Rick at last," he said excitedly.

Mother ripped the letter open and began to read. "Praise the Lord! Our prayers have been answered. Uncle Rick was converted at a revival meeting." Then she read a little farther, "Oh, good, he's coming to see us. He'll be here for supper tomorrow evening."

Galen's face was sober while Mother and Daddy finished reading the letter. He was thinking of Uncle Rick's last visit, and was not at all sure that he wanted him to come again. When Mother laid the letter down, she looked very happy, but there were tears in her eyes. Galen could not understand how she could be happy and sad at the same time.

"What does converted mean?" he asked.

Mother squinted her eyes the way she did when she was thinking. "Do you remember those old, stained pants of Daddy's that I used to make a pair for you?" she asked. "Well, it's a little like the old trousers that I converted into nice ones. Uncle Rick accepted Jesus as his personal Saviour and let Jesus clean up and change his heart. We say he was converted, or changed, when Jesus washed his sins away. He's a Christian now, understand?"

Galen nodded. "I think so," he said.

While he helped Mother get ready for Rick's visit, he wondered, *Will Uncle Rick make Janet cry? Will he tell me to scram and pull my ears?* Carefully he picked up every toy so that Uncle Rick would not trip over them.

Sure enough, the next afternoon at five o'clock, a car drove in. Galen ran to the porch, but he had to look twice to be sure it was Uncle Rick in the little, green car. His long hair had been neatly cut and combed. The straggly beard and mustache were gone. His clothes were neat and clean.

When Uncle Rick saw Galen he called, "Hi, Galen!" and jumped from the car. Pal pricked up his ears when he heard that familiar voice, then he tucked his tail between his legs and crept behind the porch glider. Tabby jumped off the porch and ran behind the garage.

Mother, Daddy, and Janet came out on the porch as Uncle Rick bounded up the steps two at a time. Hugging Mother with one arm and shaking Daddy's hand at the same time, he said, "Meet your prodigal brother. The Lord has done great things for me. I had to come and let you rejoice with me."

When Daddy stopped shaking Uncle Rick's hand, the prodigal picked up Janet and gave her a kiss on her chubby, pink cheek. No longer afraid, Janet threw her arms around his neck. Then Uncle Rick stooped and gave Galen a big, bear hug. "I'm sorry I was so mean to you the last time I was here," he apologized.

Just then Uncle Rick noticed Pal crouching behind the glider. "Come, Pal," he coaxed. "I can't blame you for being scared of me after the way I treated you." Pal wagged his tail at the friendly voice, but he didn't come out.

"Supper will be ready in about twenty minutes," Mother said as she went back into the house.

Uncle Rick turned to Galen, "Would you like a ride in my little VW before supper?" he asked.

Galen tucked his shirt into his trousers. *Uncle Rick really has changed,* he told himself. Aloud he said. "Sure thing; let's go!"

THELMA AND THE DISHES

Mother tried to get one more bite of carrot into Louise's round, little mouth. But Louise's eyes were closed, and her curly head drooped sleepily to one side. Mother pushed her chair back from the table and got up to carry Louise to her crib in the nursery.

Thelma looked at Martha. Martha looked back at Thelma. After Mother had left the room, the girls slipped away from the table and tiptoed out the back door, closing it softly behind them. Then they dashed to the woodshed.

"We made it," panted Thelma, with one brown eye peeping through a crack. "Mother didn't see us going. Now let's get up to the orchard quickly before she calls us to do the dishes."

"Good," said Martha. "We can't hear her

calling from the orchard. Anyway it isn't fair that we always have to wash the dishes, and David gets to go with Daddy on the tractor."

Thelma peeked again. "All clear," she whispered, and away she ran up to the orchard.

Martha stepped outside a moment later to follow, but as she did, she heard Mother call, "Girls, come here, please."

Slowly Martha walked to the house. "Where is Thelma?" asked Mother when Martha came in the back door.

"Sh . . . she ran up to the orchard so she wouldn't have to wash the dishes," Martha admitted.

"Well, dear," said Mother, "I am glad you didn't run away. The baby cried with colic last night, and I didn't get much rest. I need my helpers."

Martha hung her head. "I . . . I was going to go, too, but you caught me," she confessed.

"Well, you were honest in telling me about it, and obedient in coming when I called. I'll tell you what we will do. You may stack the dishes in the sink, and they will wait there until Thelma comes to wash them."

While Mother tucked chubby Herbert into his bed for his afternoon nap, Martha quickly carried the dishes to the sink. As she finished, angry shouts came from outside where Willard and Mae were playing. Mother came to the kitchen door. "Will you see if you can get those two to play nicely?" she sighed.

Martha hurried outside to see Willard

pulling on the front end of the red wagon and Mae clinging to the back of it, shouting, "It's my turn! It's my turn to ride. It is too! Let me have it!"

"Both of you sit on it, and I will give you a long ride," Martha offered. Soon shouts of laughter rang through the air. Martha pulled and pulled. She tossed back her brown pigtails and smoothed the damp hair from her forehead. At last she said, "I can't pull another step. Let's go to the sandbox and make a big farm."

The afternoon passed swiftly. Mother was busy feeding the baby when Herbert and Louise awoke from their naps. Martha went into the house to help. She built block houses, which Herbert and Louise loved to play with. Martha's dark eyes sparkled as she watched their sunny smiles chase the tears away.

By and by Mae came to the screen door. "Come out to the porch and help us play church," she begged.

"All right," agreed Martha. "You may have Betsy, the doll, for your child. I'll have Herbert and Louise for my children."

Soon the five children were busy playing on the front porch. While they were singing the opening song of their play church service, the gate clicked, and Thelma came slowly up the walk.

"Oh, let me help play church," she begged. "I will be the preacher." But Mother appeared at the door and called her inside. Thelma's brown eyes snapped as she saw the stack of dishes in the sink.

Mother's face was sober. "You thought you were getting out of washing dishes, but they waited for you," she explained. "You may do them now because you ran away."

Thelma filled the dishpan with hot, sudsy water and began washing. By this time the food had dried on the dishes. It took a long, long time to get them clean. "Children obey your parents," Thelma remembered. *Next time I will remember that verse sooner,* she told herself.

That evening the girls were late going to sleep. Finally Martha whispered, "Are you sleeping, Thelma?"

"No," replied Thelma.

"What did you do up there in the orchard all by yourself?" asked Martha.

"Nothing," answered Thelma. "What was there for me to do? There was no one to play with. The memory verse about obeying our parents kept ringing in my ears until I couldn't stand it anymore. So I came home. I heard Mother call, and I know I deserved having to wash the dishes alone."

Martha sighed contentedly and said, "You know, I've decided it's more fun to help Mother than trying to get out of work. I had a good time playing with the children, and Mother was able to rest while I watched the children. If we would be real helpers, maybe she wouldn't be tired so often. Shall we try from now on?"

Downstairs the baby began to cry. The girls could hear the steady creak, creak of the rocker and Mother's sweet voice singing to quiet the baby.

"All right," agreed Thelma. "Our big family does make lots of work, and we can help a lot too. I'm sure I'll never run away from the dishes again."

And she never did.

THE RESCUE

Dennis and Dianne were riding along with Mother on the way home from the dentist. Suddenly Dennis shouted, "Stop! Stop, Mother, stop!"

Mother slowed down. "What's wrong, Dennis," she asked.

"There's a pink bird in the road, and I think it's hurt. Please stop, Mother," he pleaded tearfully.

Mother drove slowly on as Dennis and Dianne looked back. "I see it too. Please stop," begged Dianne.

"I can't stop right in the middle of the road, children. We are almost home. I'll turn around in the drive and go back."

In less than a minute, they were headed back toward town.

"There it is, and there's another one hopping all around it," cried Dennis. "But it's a different color."

"Yes, I see," said Mother. "That's his mate, probably trying to help him. But the poor bird seems quite helpless."

Pulling off the road, Mother got out of the car, looked both ways to be sure no car was coming, then walked right out into the middle of the highway. The little olive-gray bird flew away, but the rose-colored one lay on its side, scarcely moving. Mother picked it up and carried it to the car.

"What's wrong with it?" the twins asked in one breath.

"I'm afraid he's very sick," Mother replied. "See, his legs seem to be helpless and his feet are drawn up tight. I think this wing is broken. I can feel his heart beating, but see how dull his eyes look."

"What kind of bird is it?" Dennis asked.

"It's a white-winged crossbill. See the white bars on his wings?" said Mother.

"Oh, look. Something is wrong with his beak," cried Dianne. "It doesn't fit together in front."

Mother looked closely. "That's natural. Crossbills feed from cone-bearing trees. They use the crossed bill to lift the scales on the cones and get the seeds underneath," she explained.

"Let's take him home and nurse him back to health," begged Diane.

Just then the bird fluttered and hopped down to the floor of the car. Mother stooped down and picked him up.

"Look, he's getting better!" exclaimed Dennis. "His legs are straightening out, and his feet aren't drawn up tight anymore."

"Sure enough, he is," Mother agreed. "See, his eyes are getting beady black. He looks quite alert now. But his poor wing is badly hurt. Probably a car hit and dazed him and broke his wing."

Dennis put his finger under the bird's feet. Mr. Crossbill clutched his claws around it as though it were a branch.

"If it were not for his broken wing, he'd be all right," Mother decided. "We will take him home and see what Daddy can do for him."

"I'm glad Daddy is a veterinarian. He'll know what to do," sighed Dennis as they pulled up to Daddy's office.

Daddy smiled his big, friendly smile, and his blue eyes twinkled when his family brought their patient into the office. His strong hands gently examined the hurt wing of the little bird. "I'll have to put a splint on this broken wing and wrap it so that it can heal," he explained.

Very carefully Daddy placed tiny splints on each side of the wing and wrapped it snuggly with elastic bandages. "I think the bird will be happier and recover faster in his own environment. We will put him in the parakeet breeding cage and take him up to Mr. Engle's pasture close to where you found him," he planned.

Dennis blinked his blue eyes and rumpled

his brown hair the way he did when he was puzzled about something. "But what will he eat?" he wondered.

"That's a good question," Daddy responded. "Crossbills feed on seeds. Let's gather a lot of cones from our evergreen trees and hang them in the cage."

The whole family helped gather cones. They arranged them in the big cage, then loaded it in the car and drove up to Mr. Engle's pasture.

Daddy filled all the cups with water and fastened the cage high in an evergreen tree. "Now let's walk out to the car and watch what happens," he said. "It may be that Mrs. Crossbill will come and help feed her mate."

"Peet, peet, peet, chiff, chiff, chiff," called Mr. Crossbill. Again and again he called. Suddenly a little olive-gray bird flew straight to the cage and clung to the side.

"Sure enough, there is his mate," exclaimed Daddy.

"Why isn't she a pretty red color like the male bird?" Dianne wanted to know.

"It's one of God's marvelous ways of protecting His little creatures," Daddy explained. "A red mother bird in an evergreen tree would be easily spotted by enemies."

In the next two weeks, Dennis and Dianne carefully crossed the highway every day and walked to the evergreen with the cage in it. They never could decide whether Mrs. Crossbill was feeding her mate or whether he was feeding her some of the seeds from the cones they had gathered. But the birds seemed satisfied.

On the fourteenth day, Daddy walked with them. He carefully took down the cage and opened the door. Gently he unwound the tiny bandage from the frightened bird's wing and set him free. For a minute the crossbill flapped his wings and blinked his eyes as though he couldn't believe his wing was moving. Then he hopped to a higher branch, spread both wings and soared up, up, up, to a distant tree.

The twins' blue eyes sparkled as they watched him go. "Taking care of the crippled crossbill was fun," sighed Dianne.

"I'm so glad we rescued him before a car came along and crushed him," Dennis added.

Jesus said some important things about birds—and you. Look in Matthew 6:26; Luke 12:6, 7; and Luke 12:24.

THE STRANGE STORM

Karen watched the trees swaying in the wind, and the rain streaming down the windowpane. "I may as well find something to do indoors this afternoon," she said as she reached for the little red school on the toy shelf.

Karen set the little red school on the table. Carefully she arranged the twenty plastic pupils in a semicircle around the plastic teacher's desk. Smiling down at them, she said in her pretend teacher's voice, "It's story time, children. Put your work away and I'll read to you." Then she tossed back her long brown pigtails, picked up *The Adventures of Jimmy Skunk*, and began to read.

Just then Bradley came into the playroom with his big, bouncy, orange ball and bounced it hard against the wall. *Wham!* The ball bounced off the wall and smashed into the little red school. The school upset and the twenty pupils flew in all directions. The plastic teacher lay on her back with her feet sticking into her desk.

Karen jumped to her feet. "Bradley Thompson!" she shouted. "Look what you did! Get out of here with that ball."

Bradley blinked his big brown eyes, and his mouth fell open in surprise.

Karen tossed her pigtails and stamped her foot. "GO!" she commanded, giving him a hard slap.

"Ouch!" Bradley shouted. "I didn't do it on purpose. And I won't get out. This playroom is just as much mine as yours, so there!"

With that, he gave Karen a shove. Karen tripped over her little chair, bumped her head on the table, and sat down kerplunk on the floor. In an instant she was up again.

"You're a mean meanie!" she shouted.

"You are!" Bradley shouted right back.

Karen and Bradley made so much noise that Mother came to see what was the matter. Without stopping to dust the flour off her hands, she separated the children. "Now what is all this about?" she asked.

"Bradley threw . . . ," Karen began.

"Karen hit me," Bradley interrupted.

"Hush!" Mother said. "One at a time. Karen, did you hit Bradley?"

Karen tossed her pigtails again. "I hit him because he threw the ball right into the middle of my school—just to spoil things."

Mother looked at Bradley. "Did you do that,

Bradley?"

"No, Mother. I didn't mean to throw the ball at the school. It was an accident."

"Well," Mother said, "for a minute I thought the storm had come right into the house. Now, tell me, has your quarreling and pounding each other set up the schoolhouse?"

"No," Karen snapped, and kicked the ball into a corner. "But Bradley had no business throwing the ball at my things."

"Karen had no business hitting me," Bradley complained.

"Well, well," Mother said. "You admit that quarreling didn't help. But you insist on doing it. If you can't play nicely, come with me." Mother led them to the spare bedroom.

Karen and Bradley's brown eyes grew big with wonder. What was Mother going to do with them?

Mother placed a chair on either side of the bed. "Here, Bradley, you sit on this side of the bed, and, Karen, you sit on the other side. I can't let you pound each other, but if you still feel like it, you may pound the bed. Scowl, frown, make faces, and shout at each other until you think you can play nicely." Mother left the bedroom, closing the door behind her.

Bradley looked at Karen. Karen looked at Bradley. The idea of pounding the bed and scowling at each other sounded funny. Bradley bit his lip to keep from laughing. Karen brought her fist down on the bed, but she couldn't keep a straight face. Suddenly they both burst out laughing.

Again and again they tried to frown, but each time, the frown turned into a giggle.

After a while Karen said, "I'm sorry I got cross, Bradley. Let's go play."

"And I'm sorry I wrecked your school. I'll help set it up."

Karen and Bradley skipped out of the spare bedroom and down to the playroom. "I know." Karen clapped her hands. "Let's pretend a big storm came and hit my school. We will be a disaster team and rescue the children and rebuild the school."

"Sure thing," Bradley agreed. "I'll get my ambulance and take the injured to the children's hospital."

Bradley made the sound of an ambulance as he whisked his toy across the room. He and Karen loaded the plastic children into the ambulance. They pretended other cars took other children to their homes. Next Bradley brought out his construction set. Soon he and Karen had the school set up again. Suddenly a sunbeam danced across the table. "Look! The storm is over!" Bradley yelled.

THE TWINS' SURPRISE

Leon and Linda skipped to the rabbit hutch with fresh carrots and clover for Mr. Snowflake's supper. Leon opened the door of the cage and said, "Come, Mr. Snowflake. Here's your supper." But Mr. Snowflake did not come. "That is strange," said Leon.

He walked to the back of the cage and opened the lid of the rabbit's nest box. Linda looked too. Then he dropped the lid shut, and they both raced to the house, calling, "Mother, Mother."

"Something dreadful has happened to Mr. Snowflake," gasped Leon as he burst into the kitchen.

"He won't come out to eat his supper, and there's fur all over the nest box," added Linda.

Mother pulled a pan of juicy, hot apple dumplings out of the oven and set them on the table. Then she smiled at the twins. "I think Snowflake is planning a surprise. Don't disturb him, and everything will be all right," she said.

The twins' blue eyes grew round with wonder. "What surprise could a rabbit plan?" they asked each other at the same time.

When Daddy came home, Leon and Linda dashed to the car. "Daddy, Daddy, something's wrong with Mr. Snowflake. There's fur all over his nest, and he won't come out to eat supper," they said in one breath.

Daddy didn't seem worried. "I think our rabbit is planning a surprise," he said. "We will wait till morning to give him plenty of time. Then we will take another peek."

"What is the surprise? Can't we see it tonight?" the twins wanted to know.

Daddy grinned. "When we are planning a surprise, do we want anyone peeking?" he asked.

"No," agreed the children, "we don't."

"Very well," said Daddy. "We will give the rabbit plenty of time too."

The twins were so curious they could eat only two of Mother's juicy apple dumplings for supper.

The next morning Leon bounced out of bed and wiggled into his pants and shirt. Linda bounced out of bed and slipped into her blue dress. Then they scooted down the stairs.

"May we see Mr. Snowflake's surprise now?" they asked.

"Yes," said Daddy. "This is morning. Here we go."

Mother was curious, too, so she turned the stove burners low and followed Daddy and the children outside. When they came to the nest box, Daddy opened the door. In one corner of the box was a heap of white fur. Mr. Snowflake sat close by. His pretty ears did not stand up, but lay flat down. He stamped his foot and looked very cross.

"Mr. Snowflake does not like being disturbed right now," Daddy explained. "We will take one peek and go away." He lifted some fur. The children saw eight little, wiggling pink balls.

Linda's eyes grew bigger. Leon's mouth fell open. "Baby rabbits," he whispered. "We will have to change her name to Mrs. Snowflake."

Mrs. Snowflake was worried. She tried to slap Daddy's hand with her paw. Daddy closed the box.

"Why did the mother rabbit cover her babies with fur?" asked Linda.

"She covered them to keep them warm while they are so tiny," Daddy explained.

"Where did she get the fur? And how does she know to do that?" Leon wanted to know.

"She pulled the fur from her own coat," Daddy said. "God made the animals to know how to take care of their babies. Rabbits have enough fur for themselves and to cover their young until the little ones' fur grows."

"I wish the babies would be pretty like Mrs. Snowflake," Linda sighed. "They aren't really very pretty."

Daddy smiled understandingly. "Wait a few weeks, and you may have another surprise," he said.

The next week, Daddy let the children look at the rabbits again. They didn't look like the same rabbits. White fur covered their bodies, but their eyes were still tightly closed.

Every day the children fed Mrs. Snowflake. One morning the children had another surprise. All the baby bunnies were out in the big cage, and their shiny eyes were wide open. They looked like huge, fluffy snowflakes hopping around.

The twins fed them grass. *Nibble, nibble, nibble,* their pink noses wiggled as they ate. Linda laughed. "They are even prettier than Mrs. Snowflake," she said. Leon nodded to show that he agreed.

RALPH'S REAL RIDE

Mother and Wanda were shelling peas when Ralph came toddling into the kitchen. "Walph help too," he said. With a quick grab he jerked Wanda's pan of peas off her lap. Crash! It landed upside down on the floor. Peas flew in all directions and rolled into far corners.

"Oh, Ralph! Look what you did!" scolded Wanda.

For a moment Ralph's blue eyes seemed to be growing bigger and bigger. His chubby face puckered as though he didn't know whether to laugh or cry. Then he giggled and began to prance up and down on the peas.

"No! No, Ralph," exclaimed Mother. Setting her pan of peas aside, she quickly picked him up. "Here, Wanda, take Ralph outside and entertain him so that I can clean up this mess."

Wanda's blue eyes sparkled. "All right," she

said with a tone of relief. She was glad to get outside and try out her new birthday gift, a shiny, green tricycle. Taking Ralph's hand she said, "Come, Ralph. Does Ralph want to ride on my trike."

Mother looked up. "Remember, Wanda, don't put Ralph up on the seat. Have him stand on the platform behind and hold around your middle. No seven-year-old is capable of handling a chubby little boy like Ralph on the seat."

Outside, Wanda pushed the tricycle over to the smooth drive by the garage. She stood Ralph on the platform, climbed onto the seat, and brought his chubby arms up around her middle. Round and round and round they went. Ralph held on and squealed with delight.

After a while Wanda's legs grew tired and her cheeks became flushed in the warm sun. She parked the tricycle and settled down in a shady spot on the lawn to watch Fido and Ralph playing with a red ball. Suddenly Fido saw a chipmunk running across the lawn. Like a brown flash, the cocker spaniel was after the chipmunk.

"Whaa! Whaa!" cried Ralph. "Fido wun away."

Wanda tried rolling the ball to Ralph and coaxed him to roll it back to her. But Ralph was unhappy because Fido had run away.

Ralph walked over to the tricycle and pointed at the seat. "Walph wide here," he lisped. Wanda tried to stand him on the platform for another ride. Ralph kicked and squirmed. "No! No! Walph wide here," he shouted.

Remembering Mother's caution, Wanda looked at the house. "No, Ralph you're too little to ride on the seat. You might fall," she tried to explain.

Ralph pulled and scrambled to get up on the seat. "Walph big. Walph want a weal wide here," he insisted. His flushed face puckered up, and his lower lip pushed out.

Wanda knew he was going to cry in a minute. Her forehead wrinkled with uncertainty. She glanced toward the house once more. Then tossing her pigtails back, she heaved and hoisted till she got Ralph up on the seat. The tricycle almost rolled away with him, but she managed to stop it. Ralph cheered and tried to reach the pedals with his feet, but, of course, he couldn't. Wanda stood on the platform and reached forward to guide the trike. "Take hold of my arms and hold tight, then I'll give you just a weensie, little ride," she said.

Slowly, carefully Wanda pushed the trike along with one foot. As she became more used to it, she turned down the hill where she could ride without pushing. "This is fun. Mother just didn't know how easy it would be," she told herself.

Suddenly Fido came sailing back across the fence, racing straight toward them. Wanda turned sharply to avoid hitting him. "Oooops!" she shrieked, losing her hold on one handlebar. The tricycle upset with a crash. Ralph flew clear of the tricycle and landed on his side. Wanda sprawled across the tricycle onto the rough cement, giving her arm a nasty scrape.

For a moment Ralph lay perfectly still. Then he began to scream at the top of his voice. Wanda picked herself up. Her arm smarted, and blood was oozing out of the long scrape on her arm. She wanted to scream, too, but she turned and raced to the house.

Mother met her halfway in and rushed over to where Ralph lay. "What happened, Wanda?" she shouted above Ralph's screaming.

Carefully, Mother gently picked Ralph up and examined him. Noticing that his right arm hung limp and helpless, she said, "I'm afraid this arm is broken. We'll have to take him right to the hospital. Run into the house and get my purse and several diapers while I get the car out."

Wanda was frightened. Mother wasn't even going to change her dirty garden shoes or Ralph's dirty pants.

Ralph cried all the way to the hospital. A nurse took him immediately into the emergency room. While a doctor and a nurse examined Ralph, a second nurse cleaned Wanda's arm with peroxide and painted it with antiseptic. The combination of smells and her smarting arm made Wanda feel faint.

Noticing her white face, the nurse led her out of the emergency room. "You can wait here in the lobby," she said.

Wanda half hid her face in the arm of the big chair and tried not to sob. After what seemed like a long, long time, Mother came out to the lobby.

"They are going to have to put Ralph to sleep to set his arm," she explained. "So he will have to stay here until late this afternoon. Since Daddy is on the way to the mill and I can't get in touch with him, I called Aunt Ruth to come and get you. I'll stay here to be with Ralph when he comes out of the anesthesia. Aunt Ruth will give you some lunch, and you can stay there until Daddy or I come home. Okay?"

Wanda's dimpled chin quivered, and a tear slid down over her cheek. "O . . . O . . . Okay," she stammered. "I . . . I . . . I'd rather be with Aunt Ruth than wait here."

Just then Aunt Ruth came into the lobby. Mother gave Wanda a quick hug, and said, "Don't feel too bad about Ralph, dear. He will be all right. Just try to be brave, and have a nice time with Aunt Ruth." Then Mother turned and went back to be with Ralph.

Wanda had very little to say to Aunt Ruth on the way home. Aunt Ruth had hot dogs, potato chips, and ice cream for lunch—three of Wanda's favorite foods. But Wanda's throat seemed to be choking her. She ate only a tiny serving of each.

During the afternoon she sat on the porch swing watching for Daddy or Mother to come home. While she waited, her mind was busy and full of questions. *Mother didn't even scold me,* she thought. Then she remembered that Mother didn't really know she had put Ralph on the tricycle seat.

After that, two voices seemed to be arguing. One whispered, "Don't tell her. She'll punish you if she knows."

The other pleaded, "You'd better tell her. You won't be happy if you try to hide it. Ralph might tell. Then you'll really get punished!"

"It really was Fido's fault. He made you upset," said voice one.

"But you know you could have avoided it if you had been on the seat," argued voice two.

Wanda became more and more confused. Her head seemed to be spinning.

At five o'clock Wanda saw Daddy coming. "Good-bye, and thank you, Aunt Ruth," she called and ran out to the car. On the way home, she explained to Daddy what had happened, except she didn't say that she had disobeyed and put Ralph on the seat.

Just as they reached the drive, Mother came from the other direction with Ralph. Daddy carried him into the house. Although Ralph was still so groggy that he staggered, he didn't seem to mind his broken arm. He toddled around, going from one toy to another.

Big tears welled up in Wanda's eyes as she

watched him. He looked so pitiful with his chubby arm in a heavy cast cradled in a sling around his neck. *Will he ever forgive me? Will he love me anymore?* she wondered. Suddenly she burst out crying.

Ralph looked up with a puzzled expression. Toddling over to Wanda, he stretched out his good arm, stood on his toes and gave her a juicy kiss. "Don't cwy, Wanny," he lisped.

"Why, why, he still loves me, doesn't he?" sobbed Wanda.

"Why, of course he loves you, dear. What makes you think he wouldn't?"

Wanda hid her face in her hands and sobbed. "Be . . . be . . . because it was my fault," she gasped between sobs. "I . . . I put him on the seat when he begged for a real ride. I'm . . . I'm so sorry."

There, it was out. Wanda felt better inside, punishment or not. "I . . . I know I deserve to be punished," she stammered.

Daddy's kind blue eyes looked into Mother's misty brown eyes. Mother's brown eyes looked into Daddy's blue eyes. A smile spread over Mother's face. "I'm so glad you told the truth about it, Wanda. And I'm sure you will always listen carefully now. Ralph has forgiven you, and so have we, haven't we, Daddy?"

"Yes, indeed," agreed Daddy. "Let's ask God to forgive you, too, and thank Him that neither you nor Ralph was more seriously hurt."

A smile spread across Wanda's face. She knew she was forgiven, and she felt happy inside. But it was going to be difficult to forget while Ralph carried his arm in a cast and a sling.

Christian Light Publications, Inc., is a nonprofit, conservative Mennonite publishing company providing Christ-centered, Biblical literature including books, Gospel tracts, Sunday school materials, summer Bible school materials, and a full curriculum for Christian day schools and homeschools. Though primarily produced in English, some books, tracts, and school materials are also available in Spanish.

For more information about the ministry of CLP or its publications, or for spiritual help, please contact us at:

Christian Light Publications, Inc.
P. O. Box 1212
Harrisonburg, VA 22803-1212

Telephone—540-434-0768
Fax—540-433-8896
E-mail—info@clp.org
www.clp.org